Gorillaz in the Trenches

SAYNOMORE

Lock Down Publications and Ca$h
Presents
Gorillaz in the Trenches
A Novel by *SAYNOMORE*

Gorillaz in the Trenches

Lock Down Publications
Po Box 944
Stockbridge, Ga 30281

Visit our website @
www.lockdownpublications.com

Copyright 2022 by SAYNOMORE
Gorillaz in the Trenches

This is a work of fiction. Names, characters, places, and incidents either are products of the author's imagination or are used fictitiously. Any similarity to actual events or locales or persons, living or dead, is entirely coincidental.

Lock Down Publications
Like our page on Facebook: Lock Down Publications @
www.facebook.com/lockdownpublications.ldp
Book interior design by: **Shawn Walker**
Edited by: **Mia Rucker**

Stay Connected with Us!

Text **LOCKDOWN** to 22828 to stay up-to-date with new releases,
sneak peaks, contests and more…
Thank you.

Submission Guideline.

Submit the first three chapters of your completed manuscript to ldpsubmissions@gmail.com, subject line: Your book's title. The manuscript must be in a .doc file and sent as an attachment. Document should be in Times New Roman, double spaced and in size 12 font. Also, provide your synopsis and full contact information. If sending multiple submissions, they must each be in a separate email.

Have a story but no way to send it electronically? You can still submit to LDP/Ca$h Presents. Send in the first three chapters, written or typed, of your completed manuscript to:

LDP: Submissions Dept
Po Box 944
Stockbridge, Ga 30281

DO NOT send original manuscript. Must be a duplicate.

Provide your synopsis and a cover letter containing your full contact information.

Thanks for considering LDP and Ca$h Presents.

SAYNOMORE

PROLOGUE

Trap watched as the back Jeep pulled up. He looked at Murder and nodded at him. Both of them watched as the doors opened. Don Killer stepped out the Jeep, gun in hand, as he walked up to Trap and Murder with two of his bodyguards. "Trap, Murder, I'm glad you made it," he said as he leaned back against the front of his Jeep.

"We hungry. We trying to eat like you, big bro."

"I'm glad you said that, Trap, because I have a few motherfuckers who I put on the grocery list who needs to be eaten. You get what I'm saying?" Don Killer watched as both of them nodded at each other then looked back at him. "I'll let both of ya'll little niggas know now, I don't like fuck ups and an excuse will get you bodied. So, when you cross this line, understand, the only way out is in a black bag."

"We down for whatever and we know what time it is when we cross that line," replied Trap.

"We going to see, we are going to see, baby boy." Don Killer snapped his fingers and waved his bodyguard over to him. "Yo B, give that little nigga the list with the two names on it. I want to see if he's wasting my fucking time or is they really about that life."

Trap walked up to the bodyguard and took the list from him.

"Yo, Trap, remember in this line of work you can't have no heart. It's shoot or get shot. I need that done by the end of the week. Come on ya'll, we out."

Trap and Murder watched as Don Killer got back in the Jeep and pulled off.

"Yo, Trap, whose names are on the list?" asked Murder.

"2.5 and Ammo names is on here."

"Fuck it. Come on, let's go eat."

***

The block was lit and you heard Cardi B's *Up*. You had the dice game with the homies talking shit to each other. People sitting on the steps smoking weed. You had people drinking 40s sitting on the hood of the cars. Trap and Murder walked on the block and posted up on the side of the building.

"You see that nigga out here, Trap?" asked Murder.

"Just be smooth, it's only eight. It's still early. If he's not here, he will be coming around soon."

"Cool, you post up here. I'll hit the corner store and get something to roll the bud up in. You want something?"

"No, I'm cool, Murder. I'm posted 'til you get back. I'll keep an eye on shit around here."

"Copy, I'll be back in a minute."

Trap watched as Murder walked off.

***

"What's up, beautiful? Tell me something good?"

"Like what, 2.5?"

"What you getting into tonight?"

"Shit, just chilling on the block with everyone else I guess tonight. Why?"

"Because I'm trying to vibe and just rock with you tonight, hands down," replied 2.5.

"You trying to vibe with me or trying to fuck me? Because there is a big difference in the two."

"If I was trying to fuck you I would come out and tell you, 'Yo, Shay, what's good? I'm trying to fuck'."

"Whatever, 2.5. You have so much fucking game."

"How is it game when I'm speaking the truth? Look, let's get out of here and go somewhere just the two of us where we can vibe and get something to eat without niggas in our business."

"I guess. Let me go upstairs and get my purse and I'll be right back."

"Cool, I'll be here in the car waiting on you."

2.5 sat in his car texting on his phone. The whole time he ain't see Murder sitting on the steps one building down. Murder looked around and saw a few people across the street smoking and drinking. He pulled his black .45 out and acted like he was walking pass 2.5's car. He stopped and looked at 2.5. 2.5 looked up at him.

"Yo, what's up, nigga? Your name came up on the grocery list, motherfucker."

Before 2.5 could do anything, all you heard was the blast from the .45 being let off into his car. People started running and ducking down behind cars. Murder looked at 2.5's dead body leaning over in the driver seat of the car before he took off running down the back alley.

You heard people yelling, *"They just killed 2.5."*

Trap heard the gunshots, the yelling, hurrying up off the block and called Murder. As he was calling, he saw the police cars flying down the road.

SAYNOMORE

Gorillaz in the Trenches

Chapter 1

Don Killer was at the barbershop when a few guys walked inside. "Don Killer, what's the word?"

"Shit, just watching the Giants game; losing fucking money on them. What's rocking with you two?"

"Shit, just came to get a cut."

"Well, you already know I got the best barbers in the city."

"Big facts. You heard about that shit that went down last night?"

"You already know I stay in my lane. If it ain't got shit to do with me, I stay away from it," replied Don Killer.

"I already know how you move, Don Killer AKA King of the Ville. But check this out, that boy 2.5 got clapped last night. Three to the dome, right in front of Shay spot."

"They know who did it?" asked Don Killer.

"Hell to da no. I was out there, too. That shit sounded like a three-fifty-seven; the shit he got hit with."

"Well, you know what they say, Cali. Shit happens. But look, I got some moves to make. My barbers are going to line ya'll up good and ya'll niggas stay up." Don Killer dapped them up before leaving out the barbershop with two of his bodyguards right behind him.

***

Trap walked into Murder's backyard.

Murder was sitting on the hood of the car smoking a blunt when Trap walked up on him. "Damn, nigga, what the fuck happened out there last night?"

"Shit had to go down right there last night. He was about to pull up out of there. I heard him talking to shorty about it." Said Murder.

"Niggas don't know who did the shit, but word is that his boy Ammo is going crazy trying to find out who bodied his boy. I heard he beat Shay up and everything, talking about she set his nigga up," said Trap.

"Damn, low key. That's the way shit went down. Fuck it. We got our own problems to worry about. When you trying to push Ammo shit back?"

11

"We can do that in a day or two, Murder. Let shit cool down then we can rock son to sleep," replied Trap.

"Shit, what you trying to get into now?"

"I'm about to pull up on Tasha and try to get some power mouth. I'll link up with you later on tonight."

"Copy dat."

Murder watched as Trap walked out of the backyard. In his mind, they were more than just homies. They were brothers from the sandbox and blood couldn't make them no closer.

***

"Who the fuck was on the block when 2.5 was hit? How the fuck niggas ain't see shit? This shit ain't adding up." Ammo looked around at all his boys as he pointed his gun at everyone. "You know what? Fuck it. Start free-picking niggas. 2.5 ain't dying alone. I don't give a fuck who don't like it."

"Yo, Ammo, you don't think that Don Killer had anything to do with it?"

"You know what? We might need to go talk with him to see what he knows."

"You want me to set that up?"

"No, fuck that shit. If he did have something to do with it, it's going to come to the light. I want to keep everyone in the dark like we don't know what the fuck is going on 'til I figure shit out. I want everyone on the block around the fucking clock. Yo, Little Rock, come with me. The rest of ya'll niggas hug the block until you hear something."

***

"Don Killer, I guess that little nigga wasn't just talking. The way Cali was talking, he opened his wig up."

"I see that." Don Killer sat in the backseat rolling a blunt.

"Let's see how long it takes them to push Ammo hat back then we will know what they are talking about, DJ," said Don Killer.

"So, when they pull this off, what you got lined up for them next?"

"I'll put them in the trap house until shit cool down. I'll keep them working for me. I need souljas like them. I wish I had a hundred more little niggas like them. Facts."

SAYNOMORE

Chapter 2

Trap sat in the chair smoking a blunt as Tasha used her jaws on his manhood, bopping her head to the music playing in the background. "Yo, Tasha, you are the truth. I can't lie, sexy, you be having the kid fucked up."

"I hear you like the way I be sucking that wood."

"You know I do," replied Trap. "You are too much for TV."

"What you getting into later, Trap," asked Tasha.

"Why? What's up?"

"I was hoping you would stay the night and chill with me."

"That do sound like a plan, but first I have to take care of something; me and Murder."

"So, what time you think you will be coming back over?" asked Tasha.

"I ain't going to bullshit you. It's going to be late. Probably like ten."

"Bae, that's cool. Just be safe out there. I know you heard about what happened to 2.5 last night. Niggas don't give a fuck about who you are no more."

"Yeah, I heard a little something about that shit."

"Yeah, they killed him in front of Shay's building. She said she was just talking to him not even two minutes before it happened."

Trap leaned over to Tasha and gave her a hug and a kiss on the forehead. "Look, I have to go. I'll call you later on tonight."

"Okay. I'll be waiting on your call." Tasha got out of the car and watched as Trap drove away.

***

Murder sat on the hood of his car and was looking down Smith Street when AT, a smoker, walked up to him. "Hey, Murder, you got something for twenty dollars?"

Murder looked at the dirty $20 dollar bill that AT handed him before putting it in his pocket. "You know I stay with something to hustle with," said Murder.

"You need to watch out. Murder, you know it's hot and the police is riding around, jumping out on people, looking for the motherfucker who killed 2.5"

Murder looked around. "You saw them out here today?"

"Early on Miller Ave, but that was this morning."

"Well, good looking on the heads up."

"Anytime."

Murder watched as AT walked off. That's when the black 2018 Lexus ES 350 pulled up and the back window rolled down. Murder looked as Don Killer was sitting in the backseat.

"Yo, baby boy, let's talk."

Murder looked around then jumped off the hood of his car and got into the backseat of the Lexus.

"I see you was hungry, little nigga. Why you always so quiet and shit?" asked Don Killer.

"I really don't be having shit to say," replied Murder.

"I saw you make that play just now. So, you be moving rocks, too?"

"I do what I got to do. Niggas ain't giving out hundreds in the streets."

"You right. That's why I'm glad I ran into you. After ya'll get gone with the last job, I'm setting you up in one of my houses. How that sound?"

"It sounds smooth to me," said Murder.

"When ya'll get done hit me up."

Murder looked at him, nodded, opened the car door and stepped out. He watched as Don Killer's car drove off.

"Trap, I know shit is hot right now, but we need to knock this nigga off."

Trap watched as Murder cleaned his .45 off.

"Murder, you need to get rid of that hammer. That bitch got a graveyard on it."

"Man, you tripping. This bitch is my trophy. Plus this is my brother's toy. Look, man, JRoc up north right now doing time. By the time that nigga come home, we will have him some new burners."

"But if you get knocked with that—"

Murder cut Trap off. "You sound crazy as fuck. I'm going out blazing. *Bam-Bam*! But look, I'm trying to hit Ammo up tonight and I know where he lay his head at. You down with this one-eighty-seven tonight?"

"Yeah, let's get this shit over with, homie," said Trap.

"That's what I'm talking about. Now, roll that blunt up, man."

***

Ammo stepped out of his car on Greatneck Road with two bags in his hand as he walked up to Markeys. "What's the word on the block?"

"Niggas don't know shit, Ammo. The streets ain't talking. It's like son got bodied by a ghost."

"Look, I don't care if you have to get every hitta in the Flattops on the block. I need to know something yesterday. I don't care if you have to go through the Sticks, the 40's Northside, P-Town or on Albany Ave and Smith Street. I need to know something by the end of the week." Ammo handed the bags to Markeys. "Look, you have two pounds of Gas in this bag and a brick in this bag. Let me know something by the end of the week and have my money by next week. I'm out, man."

Markeys watched as Ammo left.

***

"Man, where the hell this fool at, Murder?" asked Trap.

"Just chill and be patient. We in the cut like a band aid. He going to pull up soon, then I'll add another body to that graveyard you was talking about getting rid of. You know what's so crazy? Don Killer got us rocking 2.5 and Ammo heads off when the real nigga who runs the Sticks and got niggas pushing work on the block is Trance."

"Fuck asking questions. that's what we are getting paid for."

"That's not our job. Our job is to smoke Ammo, period. Murder, headlights, headlights."

"Yeah, this nigga is pulling up now." replied Murder.

"Who he with?"

"I don't give a fuck who he's with, Trap. Both of them is getting rocked tonight."

Murder and Trap watched as Ammo and a female stepped out of the car, walking to his front door. It was dark outside. Ammo ain't see them when they ran up on him from the side of the house, guns out.

"Bam-Bam, muthafucker! Whats' up?"

"Oh shit!" yelled Ammo as he dropped his bags. "What the fuck ya want?" Ammo said with his hands in the air, looking at the female he was with.

"Nigga, you got caught slipping, 2.5 got caught slipping fucking around with a bitch."

"Ya'll the niggas who killed my boy?" asked Ammo.

"Now you are about to go to sleep with that pussy."

Before Ammo could say anything, bullets were wrapping through his chest as Murder and Trap shot him over 10 times, killing him. Trap looked at the female on the ground screaming.

"Yo, come on, man. That bitch ain't got shit to do with this."

"Nigga, fuck what you talking about. That bitch is a witness." Murder pointed his gun at her head and shot her two times, killing her. He watched as her body fell on top of Ammo's body before he took off running to his car two blocks over.

Chapter 3
Two weeks later...

"Yo, Murder, pull up for a second. Check this out."

"What's good, Trap?"

"The streets is talking. They saying that Trance got twenty-thousand large or a half of bird on whoever pushed 2.5 and Ammo wigs back."

"Man, that shit is water under the bridge. Come on. That boy Don Killer want us to pull up at the barbershop. He needs to talk to us about something," said Murder.

"Come on. Let's see what he talking about."

***

Don Killer was smoking a blunt, sitting in the chair at the barbershop. When he saw Murder and Trap walking through the door he got up and started to clap. "My hittas, my hittas. I see you was hungry. Come to the back with me. Let me show you something." Don Killer walked to the back of the shop with Trap and Murder walking with hm. He opened a door and had 2 kilos of cocaine on the table. "What ya boys know about that? What ya see right there is sweeter than pussy. I'll give them to ya wholesale, thirty-four thousand apiece, and I'm putting ya in one of my spots where you can move it at. And I got something else for ya." Don Killer opened a drawer and handed them both $10,000 apiece. "So, what ya say?"

Murder looked at him with a smile on his face. "Let's eat."

Trap nodded. "Let's get this money, baby."

"That's what the fuck I'm talking about, my hittas. No. Fuck, my goons. Come on. Let's get ya set up at the spot."

***

Trance rode in the backseat of a Ford truck. The truck stopped in front of Don Killer's barbershop, and Trance stepped out. He looked around, took his glasses off, and started walking towards the barbershop with 3 of his goons walking behind him.

"Yo, Don Killer, you got this nigga Trance walking up in here with three of his boys."

"You know that nigga lost," said Don Killer as he walked towards the front of the shop. "What up, Trance? You must be lost."

"No, I know where I'm at. Business looks like it's going good."

"On the streets, in my shops my business is always flowing. But since you up in here, what can I do for you?" asked Don Killer.

"Since you bring up the streets, I'm trying to see if you heard anything about my two men getting knocked off," replied Trance.

"See, that's the thing. Niggas got the game fucked up. They think being a rat is talking to the police."

Trance looked at Don Killer with hate in his eyes.

"No, being a rat is minding other peoples' business and telling a motherfucker what you heard and saw. But no, nigga, I don't know shit and I don't respect the fact you coming in my spot trying me like a fucking rat. So, you need to find the door before we take it another way up in here."

"Is that a fucking threat, Don Killer?" replied Trance.

"Take it the way you want to take it and make sure you keep your niggas on your side of town— the Sticks, the 40s to Greatneck Road. And I got from the top of Albany Ave to Sunrise Highway and all the Flattops. You got me?" replied Don Killer.

Trance looked at his boys. "Come on, ya'll. We out." Trance turned around and walked off back to his truck.

"Yo, Trance, what we going to do with that nigga?"

"You know what time it is, Markeys. Call the homies up and tell them to a drive by on the shop. If he ain't kill the homies, he's going to take responsibility for it now."

***

"Tasha, what's that look on your face?"

"Kim, something just don't seem right with Trap."

"What you mean?"

"The other night we was chilling and I asked him was he going to stay with me for the night. He told me he had something to do, but he will be back later that night," said Tasha.

"So, what don't seem right then?"

"Kim, when he came in, he took off all his clothes and put them in the wash and went right to the shower. His phone went off and there was a text from Murder that said stay ducked off for two or three days and we will link up Friday and get up with D-K."

"So, what's the big deal with that, Tasha?"

"It was the same night that Ammo got killed."

"Tasha, are you telling me that Trap and Murder is the ones who killed 2.5 and Ammo?" asked Kim.

Tasha looked around her neighborhood as she sat on her steps, talking to Kim, and without saying anything nodded her head.

"Tasha, do you know how much money is on they heads right now if Trance was to find out?"

"I know this, Kim, but I might just be thinking too hard. I might just be overreacting; that's all."

"Look, just be safe is all I'm telling you. I have to go get my little brother off the school bus, so I'll catch up with you later, girl."

"Okay, just call me, Kim."

"I will."

Tasha pulled out her phone and texted Trap and said, "Call me. We need to talk."

***

Trap was counting money from the plays they were making, making sure everything was adding up right while Murder was weighing up and bagging coke. They had the homie A-Dog cooking the coke. The trap house was banging within the first 24 hours. They made over $15,000. They had brown flags hanging off the walls with B.O.B. under it. Murder spray-painted *B.R.O.W.N.S.* on the walls.

"Yo, Trap, how much bread is that?"

"This is twenty-four-thousand right here. We need another ten and the first brick is paid for."

"Shit, the way shit is going, we should have that ten stacks in no time. By tomorrow night at the latest. Big facts."

"Trap, Murder. Look, I don't know about you two, but I'm hungry as fuck. I'm about to go to the bodega. Ya niggas want something?"

"Yeah, let me get a beef patty with cheese. What about you, Murder?"

"Yeah, let me get the same thing, homie."

"Cool, I'll be back in a hot minute."

Chapter 4

"Don Killer, what the fuck that fat nigga thought coming in here asking questions? He must got the game fucked up."

"Fuck that fat boy, Little-P. He ain't talking about shit. On God." Don Killer turned around and saw the guns pointed to him outside the truck window in front of the barbershop.

As bullets started flying through the shop window Little-P, ran and grabbed Don Killer and threw him to the floor as bullets were flying through the window, hitting everything. After two minutes you heard the truck peeling off. Little-P was covering Don Killer until he heard the truck peel off. "Don Killer, you good?"

"What the fuck? That nigga just killed himself," said Don Killer out of breath in an angry voice. He looked around at all the holes in his walls and everything bullets hit. "Is everyone good?" asked Don Killer, looking around at everyone.

"Yeah, everyone is good big, bro."

"Little-P, go get everything out the back before the police get here. Shit just got real for Trance."

***

"Yo, Trap, Murder. Guess what the fuck just happened?"

"What's good, dog? What went down?" Murder asked.

"Don Killer shop just got aired out by that boy Trance not even ten minutes ago."

"Don Killer got hit up?"

"Not that I know of, but they said he is going sideways right now."

"Say, Trap, clean and wrap this shit up. We need to load up and go by the shop now."

"Yeah, we do. Don Killer just texted me. We need to go now."

***

Trap walked into the barbershop. As he looked around, he saw holes everywhere. Broken glass was on the floor. He turned around when he heard Murder walking in the door.

"Damn, they lit this place up."

"Yeah, they did, Murder, but no one was hit."

"Where is Don Killer at?" asked Trap.

"Lil- P told me he's at the other spot right now."

Murder looked at Lil-P as he came out the backroom. "What the word, Lil-P?"

"Anybody rocking with Trance, you get bodied. He don't care where the fuck you see them at. Shoot on-site."

"Copy, copy."

"Murder, we out. Come on."

"Where the fuck we headed?"

"Back to the spot 'til tonight, then we going to hit the block and put that work in," replied Trap.

"So, on some real shit, you want to hear it from Don Killer's mouth first?"

"Big facts, hands down."

***

Trance looked as the black truck pulled up on the block and both of his souljas got out laughing as they walked up to him. "How did it go?" asked Trance.

"We popped the bottle and lit that bitch up."

"Did you get Don Killer?"

"We don't know. We pulled up, sprayed the barbershop, and got out of there."

Trance walked up to them. "See, I guess I ain't make myself clear enough to the both of you before you left. I told you I want bodies and Don Killer in a black bag. So, all you two did was waste my fucking bullets by shooting up the barbershop. You niggas might as well had been shooting the fucking clouds." Trance shook his head at them. "Both of you get the fuck out my face and post up on the block. You don't know how to kill anybody so make me some fucking money." Trance walked back to the corner store inside to the back where they had a dice game going on.

Chapter 5

"Trap, that shop was lit up," said Murder.

"Yeah, Lil-P told me they shot that bitch up with AR-15s. He saw the shell casings on the ground."

"How you think Don Killer's going to come back at him?"

"Sideways. Big facts."

"You never asked yourself why he wanted 2.5 and Ammo knocked off?"

"I don't ask questions. I just got us in the door so we can eat."

"Check me out, Trap. You know that bitch Innocence lives in the new homes?"

"Yeah, that light skinned bitch that works at the strip club."

"Yeah, baby girl, you know, word is she had Don Killer fucked up. She was laying that pussy down on him. Dude was tricking off with her and word got back to him that she was fucking 2.5 and Ammo for the dollar."

"Wait, you telling me that we bodied two niggas over some pussy?"

"Dead ass, homie."

"Yo, roll that blunt up, twin. That shit got me blazing hot right now."

Murder passed the blunt to Trap. When he heard the front door open he grabbed his glock and went to look. That's when he saw Don Killer and Lil-P walking in. "What's the word, Don Killer?"

"Strap up. We riding out."

"Where we headed?"

"I got one nigga in my eyes and that's Trance."

"Let's catch the one-eighty-seven, then."

Trap looked at Murder as he walked out behind Don Killer and Lil-P. He picked up his guns and followed behind them.

***

Murder sat in the backseat and watched as Trance and his boys was outside in front of the deli.

"Yo, ya'll, listen up. I want Trance face on a t-shirt. That's the only nigga I got in my eye tonight. Let these niggas know what the fuck happens when you pull up on me and your shooters miss. My name is Don Killer for a reason." Don Killer looked at everyone. "Guns up. Come on. Let loose on these niggas."

Murder got out the car with his gun in his hand with a red flag over his face, with Trap by his side with a black flag over his face.

All you heard was Don Killer yelling, "Yo, Trance! I came for your soul, motherfucker!"

Trance turned around and looked just in time to see the sparks fly from the guns.

Bang, Bang!

Trance turned around as he fell on the ground. Murder ran up on his boy and shot him two times in the face as Trap shot the other one in the back that tried to run, killing him. Trap and Murder walked up to Don Killer as he stood over Trance.

"Yo. Killer, don't shoot, don't shoot."

"Fuck your pleas, niggas."

Trance rolled over, holding his chest. Don Killer pointed the gun at his face and shot him two times. All you saw was blood splat everywhere.

"Come on, ya. We out."

"Yo, Killer. Police."

Trap turned around and started shooting at the police car, and so did Murder. The police car hit a parked car when the officer jumped out. Don Killer shot him dead in the head, dropping him. They all ran back to the car as Lil-P drove off, getting them out of there.

"Yo, Lil-P, get rid of the car. Trap, Murder, ya'll do the same thing with the guns. Ya niggas stay low for the next few days."

Chapter 6

"Murder, this shit all over the news and in the papers. Did you read this shit yet?"

"Trap, shit was bananas the other night. I'm just trying to stay ducked off."

"Murder, we got three dead bodies, a dead cop and a cop in the ICU fighting for his life. Nigga, if we get caught for this shit, we ain't never getting out of prison. We going under the jail."

Murder sat back laughing.

"Yo, what you find funny, homie?"

"You saying we going under the jail. Nigga, please. Can you say death row? Nigga, I told you I'm going out blazing, bro; hands down."

"This nigga Don Killer just texted me and said meet him at the warehouse tonight at eight."

"Let's see what the homie talking about since all of this fuck shit happened over some pussy."

"Big facts."

***

Don Killer leaned up against his car smoking a blunt when Trap and Murder pulled up. "How ya holding up?"

"We good. Staying low like you said."

"You good, Murder?" asked Don Killer.

"Yeah I'm straight."

"So, what's the move, Don Killer?"

"See, Trap, I can't afford no loose ends. So, I got to get rid of the witness."

"What witness? It was just us and Lil-P?"

"Yeah, I know. Lil-P is dead already." When Don Killer said that, he pulled out his gun and shot Trap in the chest and went to shoot Murder, but Murder ducked behind the car.

"On God, I'll body your ass. You just rocked my twin, nigga."

"Don't worry. You going to be with that nigga in a minute."

Murder shot two times at Don Killer before running out the warehouse. Don Killer looked at him then walked back to where

Trap was laying dead with his eyes open. He got in his car and drove it out the warehouse.

Murder watched as he pulled off. He then walked back in the warehouse and was looking down at Trap's dead body. He knelt and pulled his pinky ring off of his hand and picked up his gun. "I got you, twin. I swear I'll kill that nigga. I promise you that. I love you, bro. I got to go, family. I got to go."

***

Murder sat back replaying the night over and over in his head. Now, Don Killer set him and Trap up to be killed. Even how he shot his brother in the chest, claiming his life. Looking at his brother's lifeless body was the only time he had tears in his eyes. Thinking back to that night had tears running down his face again. Murder watched as A-Dog walked up to him from the side of the house.

"What's popping, Murder? I'm sorry to hear about Trap, fam."

"Thanks, bro. Shit was foul from the jump." Murder walked up to A-Dog and gave him a pound.

"So, what's the word now with Don Killer?" asked A-Dog.

"I'll rock that nigga head to bed. It's just son is ducked off right now. Ain't nobody seen him in over two weeks."

"Word is he's in Brooklyn at his baby mom's spot, but then again you know how niggas talk, homie."

"Yo, B, look, I'm about to bounce but I'll pull up on you later, A-Dog."

"Say less. You know where to find me at."

Murder dapped A-Dog up and walked off.

Chapter 7

Don Killer sat on his desk with two stress balls in his hand knowing he was supposed to kill Murder. He didn't know how he let his little ass get away. His thoughts were interrupted when he heard a knock on his office door. "Come in." Don Killer watched as BG walked in his office. "What's the word on the streets?"

"The streets are dead right now. Ain't nobody seen Murder in the last two weeks."

"Yo, just stay on point out there. That boy got a deadly gunplay game. We might have to stop looking for him and make him come look for us."

"What you got in mind?" asked BG.

Don Killer stood up. "You know what? Let's get his attention. Set his mother's car on fire and shoot her house up. Let's see if that will get our boy to come out from hiding."

"Cool. I'll go handle that right now."

"BG."

BG turned around. "Yeah?"

"Make sure you get his attention."

"Will do."

Don Killer continued to move the stress balls in his hands as he watched BG walk out the door.

***

"Murder, you need to relax, baby."

"The streets is crazy right now, Shorty. I don't know who to trust. Shit got real over the last three weeks. Trance and his niggas got bodied, two officers got knocked off, and my twin got clapped. I might have a ticket on my head, a warrant for my arrest; shit is bananas right now. I can't relax."

Jazmine walked over to Murder and grabbed his hand and sat down on the couch next to him and was rubbing his knuckles. "Is there anything I can do for you?"

Murder looked at her and leaned his head back in disbelief from all the bullshit going on. "No, baby girl. I don't know how I'll get the fuck out of this shit, but thanks for letting me post up here on the low. Real talk."

"You know I'm here for you always." Jazmine looked at Murder and leaned forward as she unbuttoned his pants. She pulled his rod out and looked up at him as she licked all over his thick 9 inches.

Murder let out a light moan as Jazmine went all the way down on it, kissing it and sucking it as she rubbed his balls. She had Murder moaning that's how good it felt to him. "Baby, baby, damn you got a nigga ready to bust a nut. Oh shit."

"Go ahead. Bust it for me, daddy. Let me taste you."

Murder closed his eyes, grabbed the back of her head and started fucking her face as he let out a big nut in her mouth. He had his eyes closed when Jazmine tapped his thigh. When he opened his eyes, he saw the cum from his dick making a cum line to her tongue. That's when Jazmine went down and started sucking it again.

***

"Murder, wake up."

Murder turned around and looked at Jazmine. "What's up?"

"Kim just called me. She told me your mother's house was shot up and set on fire and her car was set on fire, too."

"What the fuck?" Murder jumped up and grabbed his phone.

"Murder, Murder! Your mother is okay. Kim said she might not pick up her phone. It was probably in the house. Think about it," replied Jazmine.

"Yo, these motherfuckers is dead. On the hood." Murder ran out the house with his gun in his hand. He put his black hoodie on as he made his way to the brick house. He tried calling his mother a few more times but she wasn't picking up. He made his way through the path to the back of the house and knocked on the door.

"Who the fuck is it?"

"Murder." Murder heard the locks unlocking on the door. He waited for the door to open. When the door opened he was looking at Devon.

"Come in, little nigga. I been waiting for you to come see me. What took you so long?"

"I'm hot right now and I didn't want to bring that attention to the spot. But motherfuckers just crossed the line. So, my mind is made up. There's no going back. I don't give a fuck who Don Killer think he is. I'm about to rock that pussy ass nigga," said Murder.

"Just know you only got one shot with that nigga; he plays dirty."

"Fuck that shit. Tell me how to get to him."

Devon sat down and picked up his 40-ounce of beer and looked at Murder. "Don Killer not going to have a shootout with you. He's going to stay in the cut and send his hitters. The only reason he tried that shit last time was because he thought he had you down bad."

Murder pulled his gun out and placed it on the table. "There's more bodies on this motherfucker than that bullshit graveyard down the street got in graves and I'm still adding, and Don Killer is on the list."

"I heard over an hour ago he played the game wrong and went after your peoples, so I guess you ready to break the rules?" asked Devon.

"Man, fuck the rules. On the set."

"Well, I heard he got a spot on Overland. A little white house where he keeps all his shit at. One nigga, two bitches and about fifteen or twenty of them things."

"How you know that shit is going to be there?" asked Murder.

"What the fuck? You think I'll set you up on a blank mission, nigga?"

"Naw. I know you wouldn't do no fuck shit like that. I know how you rock already, big bro," replied Murder.

"When you hit that shit up, do it around nine or ten and don't leave nobody alive in that bitch. Words going to get back to him. You going to force his hand where he wants to see what the fuck happened. Stay in the cut and wait for him to pull up, and when he pulls up, there ain't no talking. Let that four-round bark. Remember, that nigga bleed just like us. That nigga ain't bulletproof."

"Copy that, nigga." Murder got up and put his gun on his waist. He gave Devon a pound and walked out the back door.

***

"Yo, Killer, I painted that nigga Murder a perfect picture on how we get down. The shit I did, if it don't get his attention, then we might need Jesus to come down here and scream his name."

Don Killer pulled his blunt and looked at BG. "Put everyone on the block on and let them know I said shoot or get shot. I want that nigga's body in the street."

BG looked at Don Killer and nodded before walking off.

Chapter 8

Murder sat across the street in the bushes from Don Killer's stash house. It was 8:45PM. He noticed the window on the side of the house as the lights came on. He looked across the street and down the block. He ain't see nobody. He hopped the gate and ran across the street to the side of the house. He walked to the front door and knocked two times.

"Who is it?" said the female.

When the door opened, Murder put his gun in her face. "Don't say a fucking word. I will kill you. Nod if you understand." Murder watched as she nodded. "Good. Is there anybody else in the house?" Murder looked around. He ain't see nobody. He pulled the duct tape out his back pocket and taped her hands behind her back and feet together, then taped her mouth. He walked in the room and saw the other two people having sex. They were so into it that they didn't see him looking at them. He pulled his gun out then turned on the light. "Fuck up and die is all I'm saying."

"Who the fuck are you?"

"The nigga you really don't want to piss off. Now, get the fuck up," replied Murder.

Murder watched as they got out the bed. "Shorty, catch. Tie his hands up behind his back now." Murder had his gun pointed at her as she did what he told her to do. He then walked up to her and threw a shirt to her to put on that was on the floor. He then tied her up. "I'll be right back." He came back a few minutes later with the other girl. "Now, you all know why I'm here, so just give me what I want and I'll be on my way." Murder walked over to the guy on the floor and removed the tape from his mouth.

"Yo, man, ain't shit in this motherfucker."

"Cool. Say no more, my nigga," replied Murder. Murder put the gun to his head and pulled the trigger, blowing his brains out on the wall.

Both girls started crying through the tape when they saw his dead body jerking.

"Now let me try this again with you. Where the bricks at?"

"In the last room on the right in the closet. It's a hidden door in there to the right."

"I'll be right back."

Murder walked out the room to where she said the bricks were. When he opened the closet door, there was the hidden door she told him about. He pulled the 3 duffle bags out with all the cocaine. He walked back to the door where the girls were and looked at them. "Thanks." He pointed the gun at both of them and shot them in the head. He made it out the house. He put all 3 duffle bags in the car and dropped the car off by the brick house. He reloaded his gun and went back to the stash house and waited for word to get back to Don Killer that he's been hit.

***

Murder watched as the white truck pulled up to the stash house. There was only one driver. He looked around before walking into the house. Murder watched a few minutes later as he came out the house, got into the truck and drove off. He knows then that Don Killer was about to get his message.

***

"What the fuck you mean they dead?" asked Don Killer enraged.

"I pulled up to the spot like I always do, making my rounds, and Damon was butt ass naked with a bullet to the head, duct taped up and Ash and Bam were bodied the same way. I checked on the work and it was all gone. The only thing in that bitch was three dead niggas."

Don Killer kicked his chair over and pulled out his gun. "BG, C-Money, come the fuck on. Ray Ray, bring me the fuck up over there now." Don Killer ain't say a word the whole ride there.

Murder watched as the truck pulled up and all 4 of them stepped out and walked in the house. Murder put his Murder One mask over his face, hopped the gate and waited for Don Killer to come back out the house.

***

34

Don Killer looked at all 3 dead bodies laid out in a pool of blood on the floor. "BG, go check that stash again just to make sure. Ray Ray, when was the last time you was here?"

"Five. I came by to drop off two more kilos. Everything was good when I left."

"Yo, that shit is gone, Killer," replied BG.

"Who the fuck had enough balls to kill they self by fucking with my shit? Come on. Let's get the fuck up out of here."

***

Murder watched as they walked out the door. As soon as he saw Don Killer, he yelled, "Yo, Killer! What's up, pussy?"

When Don Killer turned around, all he saw were the sparks leaving Murder's gun. C-Money got hit in the neck, dropping him. Don Killer pulled his gun out and started shooting back at Murder. Murder ran behind a tree.

"Yo, kill that motherfucker," yelled Don Killer.

Murder saw Ray Ray running up and he shot him in the shoulder as he took off running behind the house. Don Killer ran to the side of the house, shooting at him. He looked back at Ray Ray on the ground and BG getting C-Money in the truck. Don Killer ran and went to help Ray Ray. Ray Ray saw Murder and pushed Don Killer off him as Murder shot him in the chest. Don Killer watched as Ray Ray's body hit the ground. By the time he looked back, Murder was gone.

"Yo, Killer, C-Money dead, bro."

"So is Ray Ray. Come on. Let's get the fuck out of here, now."

Don Killer ran to the truck and pulled off, leaving Ray Ray and C-Money laid out dead. "We got to get rid of this truck, now. Go to Maple Ave. Shit ain't adding up." Don Killer sat back thinking how he was just set up to be bodied.

SAYNOMORE

Chapter 9

Murder walked through the path behind some house. He kept looking back to make sure nobody was following him. He stopped when he felt his phone vibrating in his pocket. He pulled his phone out to see that it was his mother who texted him. He also had 4 missed calls from her. He read the text. *"Hey, baby, I called to check on you to make sure you was okay. I'm fine. The neighbors called the fire department before the house went up in flames. It's more water damage than anything. The car is totally gone. The kids nowadays have no respect for the elderly, but God kept me in his promise and protected me and my family. Call me back. Love, mom."*

Murder hit call and called his mother back. After hanging up the phone with her he looked up and saw Victory Catholic Church. Murder put his phone back in his pocket, walked into the church, sat down on the back row, and just looked at the wall with the cross on it.

"We don't really get too many visitors this hour of the night." Murder looked up and saw the priest standing there looking down at him. "Are you okay, son?"

"Yeah, I am."

"Do you have a confession you want to talk about between me, you and God as our witness?" asked the priest.

Murder just nodded.

"Come on then, my child."

Murder got up and walked to the confession booth.

"Now tell me, my child, what is so heavy on your heart that you need to get off?"

"My actions could have cost my mother her life, but God kept her."

"God will protect his children. That is His promise to us all. How did your actions affect your mother?" asked the priest.

"I killed a man. More than one, Father, and my testimonies' not over. There's a promise to Death I must keep. He's still waiting on one soul." Without saying another word, Murder got up and walked out the confession booth. He kissed his two fingers and placed them on the bible as he passed the altar.

***

Murder walked into Devon's house through the back door.

Devon was smoking a blunt, watching the football game. "You missed your shot."

"I claimed two soul and added them to my graveyard."

"You making your point by being a killer, but I can put a .45 in anybody hand and have them kill a motherfucker. This shit is deeper than roots, little nigga. To be a king, you have to kill a king. The only thing you did was knock some pawns off the chessboard," replied Devon.

"I'm not trying to be a king. This is my testimony and promise to Death, to give him Don Killer soul."

Devon got up, cut the TV off, and looked at Murder. "Stay in the cut, make your money. Stay fully loaded and be ready because he's coming. And when he do, put his blood in the streets."

"What I owe you for the info?" asked Murder.

"I'll tell you later. Now, go handle your business."

Murder walked out the back door through the path.

Chapter 10

"Don Killer, that's too much work just to be sitting on. We need to watch the corners; pay the fiens for the shit they know. These niggas ain't talking, but these crackheads going to drop the ball for the right price."

"BG and these crackheads are going to be in court pointing fingers for the right reward. Just pay attention to the flow of traffic and let the breadcrumbs bring us to the candy house. Learn the art of patience. The rabbit's going to pop his head out the hole soon. Now roll that blunt up, baby boy."

***

A-Dog was in the back of the club with a bottle in his hand, standing up, smoking a blunt. You had females dancing on the floor and niggas walking around selling pills, posted up at the bar. The DJ had the club rocking, banging Cardi B, Nicki Minaj, Remy Ma and Dej Low, letting it be known it was ladies night.

Murder walked through the club fresh as fuck in white Forces, black Polo jeans with red stitching going down the pant leg, white and red polo shirt, and a white and red NY Mets hat. He walked to the back when he saw A-Dog. "Yo, Dog, what the fuck is up?"

"You come out the shadows, my nigga?"

"Man, pass that fucking blunt; talking shit."

A-Dog passed the blunt and was talking shit while Murder pulled the blunt and poured himself a drink at the table. "What's the word, Murder?"

"Business. I need you to play the block."

"What we talking about moving?"

"Weight. Ounces, quarter birds, half birds and whole birds. You ready to make the candy shop pop?" said Murder.

"You ain't saying shit. Let's get this bread and butter, nigga."

"That's what the fuck I'm talking about, baby."

"So, what's up? You trying to fuck one of these jump offs tonight?" asked A-Dog.

"I'm straight. I just knew I could find you up in this bitch. I'm about to roll out."

"Cool. I'll link up with you in the A-M, Murder."

"Copy that." Murder took another shot, gave A-Dog a pound and stepped out the club.

Chapter 11

Murder placed two kilos down on the table next to a scale. He started breaking them down into quarter bricks and half bricks. As he waited for A-Dog to pull up he knew selling weight like this would get back to Don Killer, so he just had to be on point. He figured putting A-Dog in the trap might buy him sometime. He turned his attention to the door when he heard a knock. He went to looked and saw A-Dog at the door. "Damn, nigga. It took you long enough to get here."

"Last night was crazy. I got up with these twins and the shit we did need to be on x-videos," replied A-Dog.

"Nigga, you holding, right?" asked Murder.

"Always. You know how I get down, Murder. My buddy stay with me."

"Good because you already know the smoke me and Don Killer got going on, and I don't need you slipping, homie."

"I'm always on point. Damn, family, you holding weight like that? You got the table looking like snow mountains."

"I'm just trying to eat, A-Dog."

"You ready to open shop?"

"Let's get this money, baby."

A-Dog gave Murder a pound with a smile on his face. "Word on the block is Rah took over the Sicks and they got a little movement going on."

"You been by the spot yet, A-Dog?"

A-Dog looked at Murder as he was rolling a blunt. "Yeah, I been there two times. I just ain't know it was Rah movement."

"Yo, hold up, A-Dog. The door. More money at the door. The trap is pumping today." Murder opened the door and was looking a AT, a smoker from around the block. AT was short and heavy set and she knew how to get money from the white boys who came to the block. "AT, I see you showing love. This is your third time today, baby girl."

"Let me tell you something, Murder. You and A-Dog got the biggest drums on the block right now. I can buy a twenty from you and break it down two times and make me an extra twenty dollars."

"Word, so that's what you are here for; a dub?" asked Murder.

"No, I got fifty."

"Go see A-Dog over there. He's going to hook you up." Murder looked out the door down the block then stepped back inside and closed the door.

"AT, what's the word on the block?" asked A-Dog.

"Shit, it's hot as fuck out there. They just found five dead motherfuckers in a dope house on Overland, two females and three niggas. And the streets are saying Don Killer had something to do with Trance and his crew murders."

"Word?"

"You ain't know, Dog, that Trance had Don Killer's barbershop shot up about two months ago because them Stick niggas thought that Don Killer had something to do with 2.5 and Ammo being set up and killed?" said AT

"I heard something about that, but if it ain't about Albany Ave and Smith Street, I don't give a fuck about it," said Murder.

"So, Don Killer had 2.5 and Ammo knocked off?"

"That's what they are saying."

Murder ain't say a word he just looked at AT running her mouth off about shit that had nothing to do with her. In his mind a snitch was a snitch, whether you were talking to the police or talking to somebody else about shit that had nothing to do with you.

"Well, here you go AT."

AT looked at the gram that A-Dog gave her then back at him as he winked at her before she turned around and left. Murder closed the door behind her.

"Yo, what you think about that shit, Murder?"

"I think AT be running her mouth off too much and that shit ain't got nothing to do with us, so fuck it."

"Yo, Murder, you ever find out who bodied the homie Trap?" asked A-Dog.

"Man, that shit is a cold case. That shit is going to come to the light soon."

A-Dog pulled his phone out and it was 9:00pm. "Yo, Murder, it's nine, fam. We been posted up since eight this morning. Out of two birds and we got a quarter brick left. We need to wipe this place down and pull back up in the morning."

"Real talk, I don't like moving at night. Let's get this place cleaned up." Murder counted up $7,000 while A-Dog bagged up the last of the dope. "Yo, A-Dog, catch."

A-Dog caught the knot of money Murder threw him. "What's this fam?"

"Nine thousand dollars, baby boy."

"Say less, my nigga. Same time tomorrow."

"Copy that." Murder watched as A-Dog bounced out the door. He put the money they made for the day in a duffle bag with the last of the work and left the trap out the back door.

∗∗∗

"Yo, A-Dog. Over here, fam. Pull up."

A-Dog looked at Mo and a few other niggas out there rolling dice on the side of a pink store. "Mo, what's good fam?"

"Shit, where the fuck you been at all day?"

"Making this cake; you know how I do," replied A-Dog.

"Hold up, hold up. A-Dog, this motherfucker just got Tracey. That bitch burned you. Give me them dice. My roll. Let me show you how to do this shit. Four, five, six on the wall, niggas. Crack-head, pay me my money, and I got the bank. Now pay up. You trying to stick around an get some of this money, A-Dog?" asked Mo.

"Naw, I'm good, Mo. I got moves to make to stay up." A-Dog gave Mo a pound and walked off.

43

SAYNOMORE

Chapter 12

BG walked into the trap and looked at his two workers smoking a blunt and playing a video game.

"What the fuck? I'm paying you to get high and play a damn video game?"

"BG, the trap been slow as fuck for the last week. Niggas ain't even moving a whole brick out this bitch."

"What the fuck you talking about Style? Ain't nobody coming to cop?"

"Hell to the no. This bitch been dry. That dopehead AT ain't even been around and she good for about two stacks a week."

BG looked at the work on the table and nodded. "I'll be back. Let me go check some shit out and make a few calls." BG walked out the trap back to his car, pulled out his phone and called Don Killer.

"I hope you got some-thing good to tell me besides some more fucked up shit, BG."

"I think we might find that rabbit that's been hidden in that hole with a few carrots," explained BG.

"You think or you know?"

"I'm about to pull up on somebody. When I hit you back, I might have an address, Don."

"I'll be waiting on your call, BG."

BG hung up the phone and pulled out a Newport, lighting it before driving off. He rode around Greatneck Road, 110, the Flat-tops, Sunrise Highway and found himself coming down Albany Avenue until he saw a dope fiend named RC posted on the side of the red house where all the fiends go and smoke their dope. He pulled over, got out the black Jeep and walked up to RC. "RC what's good? What's the word on the streets?"

RC was scratching the side of his face and neck, looking around high from the hit of crack he just took. "You know people talk in the streets, BG. They tell lies on lies, minding people's business."

"Yeah, but I don't think you are going to lie to me. I need to know some information and I may be able to help you out with that itch." BG reached into his pocket and pulled out a knot of hundreds.

RC was looking at the money and started bouncing on his left leg. "What you need to know?"

"Who is pushing the weight around here, making the moves?" asked BG.

"You got A-Dog and Murder fucking with the block. They trapping out the white house on Smith, right behind the path to the school."

"You sure about that?"

"Yeah, everyone is going to them."

BG and handed him two $100 bills. "Look, keep a hundred for yourself, go buy some dope with the other, and bring it right back to me. Don't tell them it's for me. And don't take too long bringing it back to me. I'll be right here when you get back." BG watched him walk off into the white house.

***

"Yo, A-Dog, get the door. RC out there."

A-Dog walked to the door smoking his blunt as he opened it. "RC, what's good? What you need?"

"I got two hundred."

"That's what the fuck I'm talking about. Come in."

RC walked behind A-Dog to the kitchen where Murder was bagging up some work.

"RC got two hundred, Murder," exclaimed A-Dog.

Murder took the $200 and gave RC four grams. RC put the dope in his pocket and walked out the kitchen as A-Dog walked him back to the front door.

"Say, A-Dog, come here."

A-Dog walked into the kitchen where Murder was. "What's up?"

"RC was just up here like forty minutes ago. He only had ten dollars. Now he got two hundred. That shit don't sit right with me, dog," said Murder.

"You reading too much into that shit, Murder. He probably came across some sucker ass white boys and made a quick flip. That's all."

"Yeah, you might be right, hands down," replied Murder.

"Now I'm about to go finish watching the door for them boys."

"Facts, facts. Big facts."

***

RC walked up to BG and handed him 2 grams.

BG looked at the work in his hand. "They had more in there?"

"Yeah," replied RC. "A whole lot of it."

"Good. Here, you can keep this, too. Who was up in that spot?"

"Just A-Dog and Murder."

BG nodded at him, got in his car and drove off.

RC walked to the side of the red house where AT and a few other fiends were smoking dope. "Can I use one of ya lighters?"

AT handed RC her lighter and watched him put a 20 rock in his pipe to smoke it. "RC, let me get a bump for my pipe?" RC handed her a $5 piece of dope. AT looked at it. "You can keep that, RC. Let me get my lighter so I can go."

"Damn, how much you want?" replied RC, as high as a kite.

"Don't worry about it. I'll get my own shit."

RC handed AT her lighter. She got up and walked off down the block.

***

Don Killer had his eyes closed, smoking a blunt while he was getting some sloppy top from his side piece with the music playing in the background, imagining the filling when his phone went off. He picked up his phone to see it was BG calling him. "Yo, you got an address?"

"Yeah, I do, and they in there right now."

"Go make a move then," replied Don Killer.

"I'm about to handle that right now." BG hung up the phone and pulled up at the trap house where Style and Loud were. He parked the car and walked into the spot. "Ya niggas strap up. We got a move to make." BG walked in the backroom and pulled out the AR-15 and M-16 and walked back to the front. "Come on, niggas, let's ride out. It's Murder season. BANG-BANG."

***

"A-Dog, help me clean this shit up so we can get the fuck up out of here."

"I'm already on it. I got the last little bit of work bagged up already in the bookbag. I'm waiting for you to finish up the count, Murder."

"Well then we out. Count done. I'm thinking about moving the trap to another spot before the streets start talking."

"Murder, we got the block on lock, paper flowing like water. I don't know, fam."

"We will talk about it tomorrow. Go make sure the front is cool so we can step out, Dog."

When A-Dog opened the front door, he saw a black car pulling up with its lights off. He watched as the back window rolled down and the AR-15 came pointing out at him. Before A-Dog could pull his gun out, the shots were coming at him. He jumped back inside on the floor and was covering his head. As the house was getting shot up all you heard were the sounds of the guns going off. BG stepped out the car with the M-16 and was walking toward the house, shooting it up. Murder ran out the side door, shooting his .45 at BG. Loud jumped out the driver's seat and started shotting his black 9-millimeter at Murder. Murder ran back into the house and ducked behind the kitchen counter with his gun in his hand. The gunshots stopped. It got real quiet. Then you heard the sound of car tires pulling off.

Murder jumped up and went to check on A-Dog. A-Dog was laying on the floor behind the couch. "Yo, dog, you hit?"

"No, I'm good. I thought I was dead, fam. I saw the fire coming out them motherfuckers as they was spitting."

"Come on, man, we got to get the fuck up out of here before the police come."

Murder helped A-Dog off the floor, getting the bookbag in the process, and ran out the back door, hitting the path.

"A-Dog, slow down. We good."

"Who the fuck was clapping at us like that?"

"I don't know, Dog. They had the Murder One Masks over they faces, but they was definitely trying to end our careers. Look, stay ducked off until I can figure this shit out. They know who we are. We need to find out who they are. Now, it could be them niggas from the Sticks or Don Killer. We got to wait 'til the streets start talking."

"Bet. I'm about to go duck off in the Flattops," replied A-Dog.

"Cool. Stay low until I hit you back."

"Love, fam."

"Love, my nigga." Murder watched as A-Dog walked through the path.

***

Don Killer got a text to his phone and picked it up to read it. *"The movie went straight to the box office."* Don Killer placed his phone down on the table, walked to the window and looked out of it. He was going to take the streets back and body anybody who stood up to him. He was playing for keeps and he was going to let it be known.

49

SAYNOMORE

Chapter 13

Four days later...

AT saw Murder coming out of EZ Deli with a black hoodie on. "Murder?"

Murder turned around to see AT walking toward him. "Yo, AT, what's the word?"

"I'm out here trying to find some decent work to spend my money on. When are you opening back up the candy shop?"

"I don't know. Right now, I'm still trying to figure some shit out. I know you heard about what happened."

AT looked at him with a disappointed face, hoping she could get some dope. "Yeah, I did. RC was the last lucky one to get blessed. That motherfucker was putting twenty-pieces in the pipe. I'm mad as hell I missed that play."

"Thinking about it, who he made that play with," asked Murder.

"I don't know. Some tall, light skinned guy in a black Jeep he was talking to."

"Wait," said Murder. "This black Jeep, did it have black rims?"

"Yeah, black rims with red on them. That Jeep was nice."

"Yo, I have to go, but when I open back up, I got you, AT"

"Okay, I'll keep you to that."

Murder walked off, pulled his phone out and called A-Dog. After two rings A-Dog picked up. "Dog, meet me on Smith Street at ten tonight at the red house."

"I'll be there, Murder."

Murder hung up the phone, got into his car and drove off.

***

Murder watched as A-Dog came walking through the cut with his hand on his gun. "I'm over here, A-Dog."

A-Dog looked at Murder on the side of the house smoking a blunt. "What's the word, Murder, and let me hit that gas you smoking on?"

Murder took one more pull and passed the blunt to A-Dog. "Remember, I told you something wasn't right about RC?"

A-Dog coughed two times. "Yeah."

"Well, that bread he pulled up with was from BG. You know Don Killer bitch. He was down the block the whole fucking time."

"How you know that?" asked A-Dog as he passed the blunt back to Murder.

Murder took two hits of the blunt. "AT was running her mouth off about it this morning at E-Z Deli. When she told me about the Jeep he pulled up in and described, son, I put two and two together." Murder dropped the roach from the blunt on the ground.

"So, what? You think RC set us up?"

"I don't know if he did it on purpose, but his actions could have got us bodied, so that fiend is guilty in my eyes."

"So what you trying to do?"

"Your clip loaded?" asked Murder.

"Always."

"There's nothing to talk about then. It's Murder Season. I know where that base-head is posted up right now. Let's go put that fiend in a grave."

Murder and A-Dog walked behind the barbershop on Albany Avenue to see RC standing there lighting residue on a glass pipe to get high again. Murder looked around. It was pitch dark outside except where RC was standing under the light.

"So, we talking to this nigga or just clapping?" asked A-Dog.

"Nigga, fuck a confession, we blasting. Come on, Dog."

A-Dog ducked as Murder walked up to RC. "What's up pussy?" RC went to take off running when A-Dog jumped out from the side and put his .357 to his stomach. "Fucking rat." All you heard was the .357 gun blast being. You saw blood coming out of RC's back. As he leaned forward, A-Dog held him up and emptied the clip inside of him.

When RC's body hit the ground, Murder walked up to him and leaned down, stuffing the $100 bills in his mouth. "Dog, come on. Let's get the fuck up out of here before them boys come."

A-Dog looked at RC's dead body and the blood coming out his mouth all over the 2 $100 bills as he walked off.

Chapter 14

BG watched as the black BMW pulled up to the trap house. Don Killer stepped out of it with a Pelle Pelle coat on a NY Mets hat, black on black t-shirt, black jeans and black Timberland boots. B.G. opened the door as he saw Don Killer walking up the walkway to the front door. "Don Killer, what's the word, family?" said BG as he gave Don Killer a pound.

"I came by so you can tell me face to face about this action movie two nights ago that none of the actors got killed in."

"It was a shootout on Smith Street. They closed down, the money flowing this way again. Shit, it's a win-win for us," replied BG.

Don Killer had both his hands behind his back as he looked at BG. "A win-win, you say, huh? BG, how many bodies we had to lay to rest behind this fuck nigga? How many bricks of cocaine got stolen from me? So how the fuck it is a win-win? From what I see, we keep fucking taking losses. The only thing you and them two motherfuckers at the other trap did was cost me more money by wasting my fucking bullets. Ya should've went to the shooting range for that shit. It still was going to cost me money. These bum ass motherfuckers got twenty kilos of mine. Who gives a fuck about a trap house? They got my product to do it. I told you I wanted blood in the streets. I don't give two fucks about a trap house. You know the big picture you ain't seeing? He a damn witness to two cops being killed. Now, I'll say this: get me the fucking blood I'm asking for. I don't care what you got to do to get it." Don Killer looked at BG then turned around and walked out the door.

BG flipped the living room table over once Don Killer was gone. He picked up his car keys and walked out the house.

***

"Murder, what's the plan now?" asked A-Dog.

"We need to open another trap, but we have to knock this nigga Don Killer off first before he catches us slipping and push our wigs back."

A-Dog looked up at Murder from the couch he was sitting on, rolling up a blunt on the table in front of him. "What you got in mind then, Murder?"

"We need to get Rah and his crew beefing with Don Killer. This way he can get the focus off us for a while."

"Rah and his homies ain't talking about shit. I know they know Don Killer had Trance wacked and they still ain't do shit," said A-Dog.

"That's the thing. They been wanting Trance out the picture so Rah can take over. That's why there wasn't no smoke behind his death, so we need to spark the fire between them now."

"And how you want to do that?"

"Body one of his workers and make it look like it came from Don Killer," replied Murder.

"After that, then what?"

"We knock off these last twelve bricks, then we will take it from there. We just got to see which way the ball rolls."

"Fuck it. I'll put the work in tomorrow night. I know where one of his spots is so it will be smooth like butter," said A-Dog.

"Make sure they know the hit come from Don Killer."

"Copy that."

"Now pass the blunt. I'm trying to get high."

***

Rah was leaning against his old school box Chevy. It was painted candy red with rims, low profile tires, white and peanut butter on the inside with 3 TVs— 2 on the headrest and the other on the dash with red neon lights under the car. He and a few other of his boys were out there smoking and rolling dice, listening to Moneybagg Yo coming from the sound system in the car.

"Yo, Rah, I know wind came to you about the shit going down on the other side of Amityville. Niggas getting bodied, fiends knocked off with money in they mouth. Shit bananas over there."

"As long as that shit don't come over here, I don't give a fuck about it, Rock. Don Killer needs to tighten his shit up."

"Big facts."

"But shit, Rock. Let them body each other and let that money come our way," explained Rah.

"You know niggas is talking shit that we ain't pop back off on them fools who bodied Trance and the homies."

"Let niggas talk. We doing a new movement. Trance was on that bullshit. I'm about paper."

"You can't get money and go to war at the same time. Then police is going to start riding around the blocks, making shit hot. Fuck what a nigga think."

"So, when that new work coming in?" asked Rock.

Rah took a sip out his cup he was holding then looked at Rock. "It's already here, baby."

Rock smacked his hands together with a smile. "Let's get this money then."

"I'm about to pull out, Rock. I got a little jump off who's about that action ready to talk into the mic; you get what I'm saying?" said Rah.

"Do you, pimping. We will link up tomorrow at the spot."

"Facts."

Rock watched as Rah drove off looking like money.

***

A-Dog was coming out of the 7Eleven in Amityville Village when he saw Rah in his box Chevy pulling up at the Brick Apartments. He walked across the street and saw him posted up with ReRe— a little thick red bone bitch, a real hood gold digger who knew how to use her body to get what she wanted. A-Dog watched as they were caked up before she grabbed his hand and led him into the apartment and waited for Rah to come out.

***

"Damn, you looking real fucking good right now. You working them panties Re, hands down," said Rah as Re walked to the stereo and put on TLC's *Red Light Special*.

"You want me to take them off for you, baby, and show you what's under these panties, daddy?" ReRe walked up to Rah as he was sitting on the couch, sat on top of him and started kissing and sucking on his neck.

He put his hands on her ass. "Won't you take these panties off, beautiful?"

ReRe licked the side of Rah's face as she got off of him. Rah watched as she bent over taking off her panties. He loved the way her ass looked. ReRe walked over to Rah and stood in front of him. He pulled her to him and kissed her flat stomach as he pulled her thongs down. ReRe stepped out of her thongs as Rah motioned for her to lay on the couch. He got on his knees and started to eat her pussy.

"Damn, baby, your tongue feel so fucking good," said ReRe as she made her hips go in a circular motion all around Rah face.

"Damn, baby, you taste like candy." Rah had both hands wrapped around ReRe's legs with his tongue inside of her.

"Daddy, come give me that dick."

"You think you ready for it?" asked Rah.

"Yeah, I want to feel you in my stomach, daddy."

Rah got up and unbuttoned his pants. ReRe watched as he took them off. When he pulled down his boxers, she sat up, grabbed his thick 8 inches and put it in her mouth until it was down her throat.

"Damn, bae. Damn, you know how I like it." ReRe sucked it and licked all over Rah's wood. He grabbed the back of her head and started fucking her face. ReRe was spitting all over his manhood. "Baby, lay back on the couch. Let daddy get into them goodies."

She laid back as Rah pushed his whole dick inside of her wet box. "Damn, baby, you are thick as hell. This is too much dick."

Rah leaned forward and started to kiss her as he put long, deep strokes inside of her.

She wrapped her legs around his back and started to scratch his back as she was cumming. "I'm cumming, daddy, I'm cumming."

"Go ahead and cum on daddy dick, bae." Rah started to fuck ReRe harder and harder as he let off a load inside of her. "Damn, you going to make a nigga move in here, baby girl; on God."

"Hell naw," said ReRe. "Not if you think you are going to be stretching out my box like that. I like my walls."

Both of them started laughing.

"Baby, you really mean so much to me."

Rah looked at ReRe talk as she laid in his arms with her head on his chest. "You know I'm rocking with you, baby. You mean a lot to me, too. I promise you that. Baby, look on my phone and tell me what time it is?"

She looked at his phone then placed it back down on the table. "It's one in the morning, Rah."

"Look, I got to go. I'll see you tomorrow, beautiful."

She kissed him on the lips. "Okay, bae." She watched as Rah got dressed, and put on some sweatpants and a t-shirt to walk him to the front door. "You coming back over here later today, baby?"

"Yeah, after I get done handling my business, baby girl."

ReRe kissed Rah one more time before walking out the door.

Rah walked to his car door and went to unlock it when his phone went off. He looked and saw it was Rock calling him. When he looked up from his phone, he saw A-Dog standing in front of him with a black hood on and his gun pointed at him. Lost for words, Rah dropped his phone.

"This message is from Don Killer. He said what's up."

Rah watched as the fire came out the gun and the bullets hit his chest. He fell to the ground. As A-Dog stood over him, he shot him one more time in the shoulder before taking off running.

ReRe opened the door to see Rah on the ground bleeding, trying to catch his breath. "Oh my God, what the fuck, Rah?" ReRe ran outside and grabbed Rah. "Help! Help! Someone call the police, please!" She looked around. "Hold on, baby. Hold on." She tried with all she had to pick Rah up. She opened the back door to his car and put him inside. She closed the door, picked up his keys and phone, got in the car and drove off, headed to Southside Hospital. "Hold on, baby. I'll get you to the hospital. Just hold on, please."

Rah was in the backseat coughing up blood, trying to breath. Before he closed his eyes, the last thing he remembered was ReRe saying hold on.

***

ReRe looked at Rah's phone. She had blood all over her when the two detectives walked up to her.

"Rawnisha Cox?"

ReRe looked up at the two white detectives. "Yes, that's me."

"I'm Detective Green and this is Detective Moore. We understand you were the last one who brought Rahmelle Sanders here about an hour ago?"

"Yes, I am," replied ReRe.

"Can you tell us what happened?" asked one of the detectives.

"Is Rah okay?"

"Yes, he is. He's in ICU right now recovering."

"Okay, because I thought he was dead. We was at my house—"

"Not to cut you off, and where do you live Ms. Cox?"

"Amityville Village at the Red Brick Apartments."

"Okay. You can continue, Ms. Cox."

"I walked him to the front door, we kissed and he left. I was looking out the window when I saw a man with a black hoodie walk up to him. Then I heard the man say Don Killer something, something about a message. I started to walk back to the front door. That's when I heard the gunshots. By the time I got to the door the man in the hoodie was gone and Rah was on the ground bleeding."

"Okay, Ms. Cox. I need you to write a statement out of everything you just told us, okay?"

"Yes, Detective."

Detective Green handed her a pen and a notepad. "Me and Detective Moore will be right over here when you are done, Ms. Cox."

"Okay, Detective."

Both detectives walked off. "So, what you think, Moore?"

"Turf war. Don Killer and Rah's crews at war. Now we know why the house on Smith Street was shot up and Trance's killer and our boys in blue."

"Let's get some warrants?"

"Let's get some warrants, Detective Green."

58

ReRe motioned for the detectives to come back over to her and handed them the notepad.

"Thank you for your cooperation, Ms. Cox." Both detectives walked out the hospital.

Once they were gone out of the door, Rock walked up to ReRe. "Yo, ReRe, tell me you ain't tell them pigs what the fuck went down tonight?"

"Yes, I did. They came to question me. What was I supposed to do?"

"Tell them you don't know and ask for a damn lawyer. You know what you just did? You put us under the gun shit."

ReRe looked at Rock as he walked off out of the hospital.

SAYNOMORE

Chapter 15

Rah opened his eyes to see IVs in his arm. His chest hurt and his body was stiff. His mouth was dry, and it hurt when he tried to breathe. The room door opened and he saw Rock coming in.

"Oh shit, you up. Let me get the nurse."

After 20 minutes the nurse and the doctor let Rah and Rock talk.

"What the fuck happened? How the fuck you get caught slipping?" asked Rock.

"I don't even know how he knew I was there. I came outside and the nigga said, 'Don Killer has a message for you,' then he clapped me. The next thing I know I'm waking up here."

"Well, shit is crazy on the block right now. The police hit two of our spots and caught a few homies down bad with the hammers on them. It's hard for us to move right now and Don Killer got locked up, but word is he's out on a fifty-thousand-dollar bond. Word is that you are a rat. You told on him and got his spots raided."

"What the fuck? Hell naw. Where is all of this shit coming from?" asked Rah.

"Your girl ReRe gave them boys the run-down of everything that happened the night you got caught down bad. I witnessed her writing a statement and all."

"Damn, I got to get the fuck up out of here How long I been here for?"

"About four days now," replied Rock.

"I know she didn't do that police ass shit."

"Yeah, she did. Word for word. I was two seats behind acting like I was on my phone. When they pulled up on her, I heard everything word for word, Rah. She gave them all details to what went down."

"Where my car at, Rock?"

"I got it at the spot, and you got your clothes over there in the bag with your phone."

"Look, I can't get discharged for twenty-four more hours. I got a lot of shit on my mind right now, so I'll hit your line when I'm ready for you to come get me."

"Copy that." Rock got up out the chair and gave Rah a pound before leaving the hospital room.

Rah just closed his eyes, thinking about his next move.

***

A-Dog was smoking a blunt, sitting on the hood of his car when his phone went off. He saw it was Murder calling him. "What's the word of the day, my guy?"

"Paper chasing. Pull up at the spot on Bayview. It's time to get this baby love again."

"Word, word. That's what I'm talking about. I'm about to roll through now."

"Say less. I'm already in the cut, son."

A-Dog hung up and jumped off the hood. He threw his blunt on the ground as he got in the car and drove off, playing Lil Baby's *Pure Cocaine*.

***

"Don Killer, the block is blazing hot right now. Three of our spots been ran in by the jump out boys, and they ain't letting off the block. It's hard to get paper right now."

Don Killer sat down in the chair, smoking a cigar, listening to BG talk about the bullshit going down on the block. "Any word from the nigga Rah?"

"Not yet, but word is you sent the shots to his head, so we don't know how that shit is going to turn out," replied BG.

"I ain't send my hitta at him. Somebody trying to get us to go at each other and it's costing me more fucking money," said Don Killer.

"So how you want to play this shit out?"

"I need to talk with this nigga Rah."

"Don Killer, I don't know about that. One dude just got hit five times, damn near bodying him. He might not be trying to talk right now."

"He'll talk. Just give it a few days until then. Just work the phone to make the plays to keep the bread coming in."

"Copy that. I'll go let the team know now."

Don Killer watched as BG walked out the house.

SAYNOMORE

Chapter 16

"Damn, it's about time you got up out that hospital, taking a damn vacation while we bleed the block and watching out for them boys."

"Whatever, nigga. You get popped five times then tell me it's a vacation, nigga."

"Whatever Rah. We out. Where you trying to go?"

"You strapped, Rock?"

"I stay strapped. Why? What you thinking?"

"Take me to go see ReRe?"

"You sure you want to do that?"

"It's nothing to talk about, Rock."

"Say less. It's your call, homie."

For 20 minutes Rah ain't say a word as they rode to ReRe's apartment. He sat back as he thought about the night he got shot. Hands down he loved ReRe but the bitch broke the rules. Rock pulled up at ReRe's spot and looked at Rah. Without saying a word he handed Rah his 9-millimeter. Rah looked at him, took the gun and stepped out the car. He walked up to ReRe's door and opened it. She was standing in the kitchen, looking at him. When she saw him, she ran and gave him a hug.

"ReRe, do you know what you did?"

"Yeah, I got your ass to the hospital. I saved your life. You coming up in here with an attitude."

"You fucking right I have an attitude. You wrote a full statement to the police. My spots been getting raided, my solja locked up and my name been assassinated in the street."

"Rah, do you fucking hear yourself? Matter fact, just get the fuck out of my spot."

Rah turned around and acted like he was about to walk out and turned around and pulled his gun out on ReRe.

"Rah, are you for real? I love you."

"I love you too, Rawnisha," Rah said as he pulled the trigger, shooting her 3 times in the chest, killing her. "Fuck, fuck," Rah said as he walked out of her apartment back to the car with Rock.

***

"Murder, murder was the case they gave me," A-Dog was rapping as he walked up to Murder and gave him a pound.

"You ready to get this baby love, A-Dog?"

"You know I'm ready to eat."

"You never told me how you caught son slipping like that," said Murder.

"Wrong time, wrong place and I just laid. When he came out, I pulled up on him like, 'Don Killer got a message for you.' Bang, Bang."

"You did that one, hands down. Come on. I got the work in the backroom. Let's start breaking this shit down."

"I'm right behind you, fam."

"Look, we going to break up the work here and bag it up, and you know that ran down bando next to the junior high school?"

"Yeah, on the first dead-end."

"Yeah, we going to move out there so the smokers can get to us without being on the main road."

"How much we going to have in the spot at a time?" asked A-Dog.

"A half kilo until shit cool down."

"Cool. Say less. Now let's get this shit bagged up."

***

Robin sat on the side of the red house called Jasse's Park. She put her rock in her pipe to smoke.

AT walked up to her. "Robin, who got rocks over here?"

Robin blew the smoke out of her mouth. "A-Dog and Murder back on."

"Where they at?"

"In the first cut by the junior high school in the white house. And let me tell you, ain't shit change. I just hit this shit and I'm already on the moon, girl. And they are doing the dollar right."

AT walked through the path holding a $20 bill in her hand going to see A-Dog and Murder. When she walked up to the white house, she looked round before knocking on the wooden door. She knocked two times before A-Dog opened the door.

"AT, what's the business, baby girl?"

"You are the business, dog. Ya opened back up the candy shop and ain't let me know. Got a bitch walking all the way down Great-neck Road for a rock not even worth smoking."

"Yo, step in. What you trying to cop?" asked A-Dog.

"I got twenty dollars. That's all I got right now."

"You know your money gold up in here. Let me go get that for you. I'll be right back."

AT looked around the old broken up house and was thinking about how it used to look back in the day.

Murder walked up to her and handed her two $20 drums. "Yo, let your people know we working out of here now."

"I got you, Murder. Looking good, too."

"No problem." Murder watched as her left out the door. "Yo, Dog, you think we might have opened back up too soon?"

"Hell no. We opened back up at the right time. We getting this paper again."

"You right, my nigga. I'm just tripping." Murder walked back to the backroom to finish counting up the money for the day.

SAYNOMORE

Chapter 17

Rah sat in the back of the club drinking shots of Ciroc, bopping to the music, chilling with Rock and a few members from his crew.

"Rah, I ain't going to lie, bro. When I got that call two weeks ago saying you got clapped, I dropped down to my hands and knees and prayed to God that you was alright. I don't care what nobody say. Prayer works."

Rah took a shot of his Ciroc. "Look, Rock. Dead ass, I thought I was gone, but that's the past. We here now, popping bottles, enjoying the fruits of our labor, living in the lime life."

"Facts. We balling. Yo, Rah, I know I ain't tripping."

"What you talking about now, Rock?"

"Look over there at the bar. Baby girl with the pink and white on."

Rah looked at the light skinned female sitting at the bar waiting for her drink, looking like a cover girl. "Damn, who the fuck is she?"

"That's Don Killer bitch, Monay," replied Rock.

"Word."

"You thinking what I'm thinking, Rah?"

"And what you thinking about, Rock?"

"Kidnapping the bitch."

"Fuck no. We ain't on no mafia shit. Post up. I'm about to pull up on her." Rah got up and walked over to the bar where Monay was waiting on her drink. "Excuse me, do you mind if I take a seat next to you, if it's not a bother to you?"

Monay looked at Rah from his jet-black curly hair, white smile and how well he was dressed. "No, I don't mind at all."

"So, let me introduce myself. My name is Rahmelle."

"Hello, Rahmelle. My name is Monay."

"Monay, that's a beautiful name. I like."

"Thank you, Rahmelle."

"Your drink, ma." The bartender handed Monay her drink then walked off.

"Well, Mr. Rahmelle, my drink just came so I'll go back to my table now."

"Are you sitting alone or would you like some company?"

"I was sitting alone, but you can come over to the table. I like your vibe, and your conversation is different."

"Okay. Let me order my drink and I will be right there." Rah watched as Monay walked back to her table. "Bartender, let me get a gin and juice on ice."

"Sure, coming right up."

"Aya, you don't mind me asking what is a beautiful female doing here by herself?"

"What makes you think I'm by myself?" replied Monay.

"I just don't see nobody with you, that's all."

"I am by myself. I'm not one to be around a crowd."

"I respect that. I do and I like the vibe that's coming off you as well."

"So, are you from around here, Rahmelle?"

"Yeah, I am. I lived in Amityville my whole life. What about you?"

"Yeah, I'm from Amityville, the northside. So, let me guess. You are a drug dealer?" asked Monay,

"If you mean by standing on the corner, selling drugs, no. That's not me, Monay."

"So then tell me what it is you do then, Rahmelle?"

"I'm a product of my own environment. I got a few guys that work under me. I'm not going to lie to you. I'm not flashy with it. It's all I know."

Monay respected his honesty and how truthful he was. "I like that you are direct and honest. You don't see that in a lot of men nowadays."

"Monay, I really do like your conversation. Can we exchange numbers?"

"Yeah, we can."

After they exchanged numbers, they talked for about 20 more minutes before Monay left with a promise she will call him this week.

"Damn, nigga, you was over there caked up like that was your boo or some shit."

"Let's just say it's something in the works, baby boy. Come on. Let's roll up out of here."

***

Murder walked into Victory Catholic Church and up to the altar. It was quiet. Nobody was in there. He made a cross on his chest then touched the altar.

That's when Father Rhodes walked up behind him. "I prayed to God the last time you were here and asked him to let your heart lead you back through these doors again. Do you wish to go to the confession booth and talk?"

Murder looked at Father Rhodes and took a deep breath. "Yeah, I would, Father. I have been to this church many times and watched the loved ones of my friends cry over they sons', brothers', cousins' dead bodies in the casket right in in front of the alter. When I come inside this church, I feel that they spirits is with me."

"It's God's presence you feel that is with you, young man. He's with you all the time, watching over you, protecting you. Every saint has a past and when you ask forgiveness and you are Catholic, you are born a new man in Chris and your past is forgiven, my child."

"Father, for the things I have done, I know there is a place for me in hell already picked out for my past deeds and sins I haven't confessed to."

"It's not too late to walk away from the path you are walking down now and start walking down the road of salvation."

"Father, I would like to make an offering to the house of God tonight."

"And your offering would be accepted in the eyes of God."

Murder placed $5,000 in the window as he passed it to the priest. "I have to go, Father. I hope my sins are forgiven one day. I still owe Death two souls." Murder got up and walked out of the confession booth, not saying another word.

Chapter 18

Don Killer sat in the car at the warehouse with BG as he waited for the dock's doors to open to go see Omaar.

"What's taking this motherfucker so long?"

"Chill, BG. Look, the dock doors are opening up now." Don Killer drove his black BMW through the dock's doors. Once the doors were closed, he and BG stepped out of the car. "Mr. Omar, it's good to see you again."

"Likewise, Don. My apologies for the wait. I had to make sure you weren't being followed for my safety."

"And why would I be getting followed?" asked Don Killer.

"Let's not kid ourselves, Don. You are hot right now. The police are cracking down on you and your crew. It's all over the news and in the papers about the raids."

Don Killer looked at Omar with his tailored suit on, down-playing him like he couldn't control the streets of Amityville. "I have everything under control on my side, Omar. I can ensure you that."

"I hope so for the sake of our relationship because I don't need no heat on me and my assets over dealings with you and your mess."

"That won't be an issue on your end. You have my word."

"That's all we have as men is our word, Don. Now that we cleared that up, shall we do business?" asked Omar. "I take it you have the money?"

"I always have the money." Don Killer looked at BG as he passed Omar's people the book bag. "Five hundred thousand in cash like always."

Omar looked inside the book bag and nodded to his men to hand the two duffle bags over to Don Killer. "Don, I do enjoy the pleasure of your business like always, but this will be the last transaction until things cool down on your end. Some risks, no matter how great the reward is, just ain't worth talking about. And in a nutshell, you are one of the risk that I'm not willing to take. Don't contact me. I'll reach out to you."

Don Killer ain't say a word as he watched Omar and his men get into their cars. He placed the duffle bags into the trunk of the car and pulled off thinking about how this cracker tried him. "BG, I need you to stretch all the work out. It's twenty birds. Stretch them to thirty. I don't know when this cracker going to call me, and we can't afford to lose no more money."

"I'm on it, bro. I'll get to work on that, ASAP."

***

Rock walked downstairs to the basement, smoking a blunt. When he turned the corner to the basement steps, he saw Rah sitting on the pool table with his phone in his hand, talking with a few members from his crew. All eyes were on Rock when we walked up.

"It's about time you got here, Rock. Pull up a chair."

Rock sat in the corner chair still smoking his blunt, looking at Rah.

"Rock, this is what's going down tonight. Word got back to me that Don Killer going to be at the block party on Avon. I think it's about time we send that nigga back his message."

"We need to be in the cut, ducked off, because if word gets out that we are there, they going to be on point and might catch us down bad, Rah."

"That's why there's only four of us in this room right now. When we pull up, we ain't doing no talking. The only thing I want this nigga to hear is, 'Don Killer, Ra told me to return this message.' And I want niggas to hear the boom when he see the sparks. If you can get close enough, dome check him," said Rah.

"What time you trying to ride out?"

"Shit, now that you are here, let's go, nigga. We been on your time."

"Let's roll out then, and take care of the business."

***

The block was lit. Music was blasting, dice game was on the wall, cars were doing burnouts. Females were dancing, the weed smoke was in the air, and dudes were battle-rapping. You had food on the grill. The block was live with everyone out there. You saw Don Killer's Benz coming down the block with him in the passenger seat, with leg hanging out the window showing off his white Air Force Ones as he smoked his cigar.

"Don Killer, this shit is lit out here tonight. I know I'll get me a bitch tonight for the sloppy toppy."

"You too much, BG. Pull up over there. We going to post up on that part of the block."

You had females and dudes walking up to Don Killer, showing him love as he stepped out of the car.

"He's the motherfucker, Don Killer. What it been like, fam?"

"You know I'm in the cut, Philly. What's the word? You looking like money, baby boy."

"Come on, man. We all trying to eat. When I pull up in something like you, then you can say I'm getting money."

"Say, Philly. Who's baby girl over there? She tough like Nicki Minaj."

"Yo, that's Candice, and don't none of these niggas got her on they hit list. That's a new breed of bitch. She ain't going for nothing."

"I'll have to pull up on that before the night is up. But look, let me holla at you for a minute. Check me out. I know you heard about the bullshit between me and them Stick and Forty Dog niggas?" said Don Killer.

"Yeah, I heard you sent Rah a message— five shells to the chest."

"Look, I'll handle that situation. That's water under the bridge, but what I need from you is to push this work on the block for me. Forty's too hot for me and my team. You do this for me and we both can get some money out here."

"I'm all for it. When you trying to do this?" asked Philly.

"I'll have BG pull up on you this week and we will take it from there."

"Say less."

"I'll go get me a drink. I'll pull up on you in a minute." Don Killer dapped Philly up before walking off.

***

"It's a hundred motherfuckers out here tonight, Rah. This nigga could be posted up anywhere out here."

"It's called the waiting game, B. So just keep your eyes open for the fool because just how we looking for this nigga, he could be looking for us." Rah sat in the backseat of the Toyota looking at everything that was going on around him, not taking his focus off of what he came there for. He wanted to show Don Killer shit was real between them and he wasn't going to lay down.

***

"Kim, look at you, looking like Aaliyah with your sexy ass."

Kim looked at A-Dog sitting on the steps with a 40 in his hand, smoking a blunt. "What's up, A-Dog? I see you stay getting blazed."

"I'll get lit until the road comes to an end for me."

"Shit, can a bitch smoke with you?" asked Kim.

"You know that's without a question. Come sit down next to me."

"So, I ain't been seeing you around. Where the hell you been lately?"

"I been fucking with Murder, running this check up. You know paper comes before all other shit," replied A-Dog.

"Ever since they found Trap body, Murder been fucking with nobody. We don't even see him no more."

"That shit really got to him. How Tasha take it?"

"She was hurt at first but she understand that was the life he was living."

"This life is a gift and a curse. The real die young and the fuck niggas live forever and a day. But look, I been trying to vibe with you for a minute, beautiful."

"A-Dog, whatever. Pass the blunt."

A-Dog started to laugh as he passed her the blunt.

***

"Say, Rah. Ain't that the pot of gold at the end of the rainbow over there with the black boomer on?"

"Yeah, that's that fool over there. Come on. Let's see if his blood's green." Rah stepped out the car and leaned against the hood of it as he watched BG walk up the sidewalk and his other soulja walked on the other side of the street. He had his hand on his gun under his shirt as he watched the play go down.

"Say, Don Killer." Don Killer turned around and looked at Rock. "Rah said return to sender, nigga."

Before Don Killer could react, Rock was letting shots off at him. He went to turn around and got hit in the shoulder. He went to run across the street, that's when he saw the man on the sidewalk pointing another gun at him, shooting. Don Killer pulled his gun out and started to shoot back as he ducked behind the car in front of him.

***

"Oh, shit! Niggas are trying to clap that boy Don Killer. Kim, get down over here behind me. They getting loose out here. Come on, baby girl, bullets don't have no name." A-Dog grabbed Kim's hand and pulled her with him as they ran off the block to his car.

***

Rock started running up the block, shooting at BG, yelling Don Killer's name. Rah ran up behind BG and smacked him in the face with the 9-millimeter, dropping him. BG hit the ground as Rah was over him, smacking him in the face over and over again. BG's gun slid under the car when he fell.

Rah stood up and looked down at BG's bloody face. "Yeah, nigga. Shit real," said Rah as he shot BG two times in the chest. That's when he saw the black Toyota pull up.

"Come on. Them blues is coming."

Rah ran to the car and jumped in. So did Rock and Tuggy. All you saw was the black Toyota pull off the block.

Don Killer got up from behind the car, holding his shoulder. He looked and saw BG laid out. He ran to him when he saw him coughing up blood. "BG, get up. We got to get the fuck up out of here before the boys come."

"Go, go. I'll be good, Don. Get the fuck up out of here before you get caught up, Don," BG replied.

"Fuck." Don Killer took off running to his car and floored it out of there.

Chapter 19

"Kim, you good?"

"Yeah, I am, A-Dog. Thank you for getting me out of there."

"You know I got you. That shit got crazy dumb fast."

"I know. I think Don Killer got shot. They was trying to get that boy."

"I saw that. Where you want me to drop you off at, baby girl?"

"How about I just hang out with you tonight?"

A-Dog looked at Kim then smiled. "Yeah, that's cool. I have to go by the trap. You cool with that?"

"Yeah, I am."

***

Rah stepped out of the car, looked at his team and nodded at all of them. "Now that's what the fuck I'm talking about. Now let the streets talk. When we pull up, it ain't no talking. Niggas want smoke then we are going to burn down the block. Ya twon burn the car. Rock, I saw you let that bitch work."

"Come on, Rah. You know my gun game is A-1. I don't do too much talking when it's go-time."

Rah looked around the garage at all 3 of his boys. "Real talk, and this is a true story, ya all did ya thing tonight. Now the streets know when it's time to get active we on go. Ya go take care of the car. Rock, go make sure everything else is good with the two traps we running out of right now."

"Say less. I'll link up with you tomorrow and let you know what's what."

"Cool." Rah dapped Rock up before getting into his car to leave.

***

Monay got out of the bed and put on her robe and house shoes. She walked down the stairs as she called Don's name because she heard noises coming from down there. Once she reached the bottom step, she saw Don Killer sitting at the table with a bottle of E & J taking shots. He had blood all over his clothes. "Oh my God, what happened to you, Don?"

"I been shot. Someone tried to kill me."

"You need to get to the hospital. Let me get my car keys."

"No, I'm good. It's a flesh wound. It went in and out. I'll live," replied Don Killer.

Monay sat at the table with him. "Where was you at?"

"The block party on Avon."

"You know, I don't get you, Don. You know you hot right now. The police are looking for any reason to kick in the door. You beefing with these so called niggas on the block, but you still got to go out and show your face like you can't be touched. Newsflash, Don, your ass bleed just like everyone else that. Bullet in your shoulder is proof."

"Hold the fuck up, bitch. You wasn't saying that shit when I put you in this big fucking house. Don't tell me how to live my life or how to move in the streets. What the fuck you brung to this table, Monay?"

"Nigga, I'm the one who got this shit off the floor. I'm the one who introduced you to Omar and got you off the corner. So, who really got this house?"

"And I'm the one in the streets taking risk everyday while you getting your hair done, nails done, living this Barbara fucking life."

"You know what? Fuck you, Don. Just keep living your gangsta fucking life 'til you are on somebody shirt."

"Bitch, did you just wish death on me?"

"No, nigga, you wishing that on yourself, Mr. Bulletproof. Oh no, my bad, you bleed, nigga."

Don Killer got up and smacked her so hard she fell to the floor. Monay touched her lip as blood was coming from it. Don Killer stood over her. "I don't know who the fuck you think you are talking to, but you better calm that shit down."

"Fuck you, nigga." Monay jumped up and started punching Don Killer in the head and trying to kick him.

Don Killer punched Monay so hard in the face she fell on the floor. She was so dizzy. He then walked over to the table and picked up his bottle of E & J and started pouring it on her. "You ain't shit but a cheap drink, bitch. I wouldn't even waste a bottle of Ace of Spades on your bum ass."

Monay looked up at Don Killer as he walked out the door. She stood up and sat at the table as tears were in her eyes, thinking about how he just disrespected her to the fullest. Monay got up and walked upstairs and looked in the mirror at her face turning black and blue.

***

A-Dog pulled over three houses down from the trap. "Come on, Kim. It's this way."

"So, this is where you be at?"

"Yeah, it's ducked off and it's not in the open. Plus, we can see who is coming from the top of the road."

Once they walked into the trap house, Murder walked out the backroom, smoking a blunt. "I see what you been doing all night. What's up Kim?"

Kim walked up to Murder and gave him a hug. "I'm good, Murder. How the hell you been?"

"Living, chasing a dollar. You know how that goes."

"Murder, it went down on Avon. There was no talking," said A-Dog.

"What you mean it went down?"

"Rah pulled up with the hit squad and was dumping on that guy Don Killer. He wasn't trying to do no talking."

Kim looked at Murder. "Yeah, somebody yelled to him, 'Rah said return to sender.' That's when I saw Don Killer get shot in the back and A-Dog got me up out of there."

"I tried to tell niggas Rah about that life and you know this, A-Dog."

"That's why me and baby girl got up out of there. I told her bullets don't got no name."

"Copy that one. Look, it's late, dog. Help me clean this shit up so we can get up out of here. Kim, you good while we handle business in the back?" asked Murder.

"Yeah, I'm good, Murder."

"Cool. Come on, A-Dog. "A-Dog and Murder walked to the backroom. Once out of Kim's sight Murder dapped A-Dog up. "Yo, Dog, that shit panned out just right."

"Big facts. I saw that by Don Killer hitting the ground. On gang."

"I still got Don Killer on my hit list if Rah ain't body him."

"Well, let's get this shit cleaned up and see what the streets is talking about tomorrow, Murder."

Chapter 20

Monay woke up the next morning and walked into the bathroom. She looked into the mirror. Her eye was swollen where Don Killer punched her and so was her lip. She had black and blue marks on her face. As she looked at her reflection, tears rolled out of her eyes. She walked back into the bedroom and packed all her things up. She had a stash of money she'd been putting up over the years. After getting dressed she put all her things she could carry in her Lexus and left. She promised herself she would never let a man hit her, and if one ever did, she would kill him. And Don Killer was going to pay for putting his hands on her. "He beat up the right bitch this time," she said to herself.

***

Murder pulled up to A-Dog's spot and stepped out of the car. He looked around before walking to his door. He knocked two times before A-Dog opened his front door. "Top of the top, fam."

"Top of the morning, bro. I'm glad you stopped by. There've been some things on my mind since last night."

"What's good, A-Dog?"

"Come in the living room and have a seat, bro."

Murder sat down on the loveseat and leaned back, looking at A-Dog. "Murder, we been piped up in these streets the last few months on a crazy body count. The streets is hot right now. We caked up for real, bro. We need to sit back and enjoy the fruits of our labor and let Don Killer and Rah body each other. It's wicked out there right now. Murder, I'm not saying leave the streets alone, I'm just saying let's fall back for a minute, bro."

"I feel you, A-Dog, but I was there when Trap got killed. I was there when he got shot in the chest. I was there when he took his last breath. I saw the look in his eyes before he died. There is no slowing down for me, There's no turning back for me until Don Killer is dead. And I'm not even sure I'll stop then. So, if you want to call it quits, respect and love, but there is no stopping for me right now. I'm all the way in."

A-Dog looked at Murder and all he could do was respect his mind frame. Murder was loyal to the streets, but the game wasn't loyal to him. Now he was breaking the rules as he played the game, just as the game betrayed him. "I'm with you, Murder. I'm all the way in. I ain't know you was there when Trap was killed. I know that was your ace and you brung me to the table to eat with you. So, if they kill you, they kill me, my nigga. I'm all the way in."

Murder dapped A-Dog up. "Love, homie."

"Always, Murder."

***

Don Killer sat in the back of the barbershop. His arm was in a sling. The barbershop was closed as his crew was standing around, waiting for him to talk. "Last night Rah and his boys tried to kill me. The bullet that went through my shoulder is proof. And BG is laid up in the hospital with tubes down his fucking throat, fighting for his life. This shit ain't going to go unanswered. I want blood in the fucking streets behind this. I don't give a fuck if the bullets hit women and kids."

"Say, Don Killer, what about the trap houses?"

"Everything goes on pause right now. Remo, we going to show them what beef is. Play the blockm and when you find out where he's atm let me know before anybody makes a move. Do I make myself clear?"

Everybody nodded.

"Good. Don't nobody call me until you know where this fuck nigga is. Now get out my face."

Don Killer looked at everyone leave. He was mad they caught him down bad like that, but he said to himself they fucked up and ain't kill him. They shooters missed but his won't.

Chapter 21

"How we looking over there, Murder?" asked A-Dog as he was weighing up the coke and breaking it down.

"We getting low, A-Dog. We down to the last five kilos. We need to reup before we run out."

"We can pull up to Omar garage. He only deals with weight."

Murder took off the rubber gloves and walked over to the table where A-Dog was sitting, eating a slice of pizza. "You know that cracker like that?"

"I know of him and what he do, but I don't know him personally."

"How you think that's going to look if we roll up on him trying to shop out the blue?"

"You got a better idea?"

"Yeah, I was thinking about them Riverside niggas."

"We are going to end up killing one of them for playing games. I say we just pull up on Omar and put our cards on the table. And it's not like we coming to him with two or three grand. We pulling up with a hundred and fifty-thousand so we might walk out of there with three and a half birds."

"Fuck it. When you trying to pull up on him?"

"Between three and five, so it ain't too early in the day or late in the afternoon. And we need to go with all big bills so it's easier for us to cart."

"Big facts. Come on. Let's count this shit up. We only have two hours before five o'clock." Murder went to the backroom and started pulling money out the safe so they could count it up.

***

"Yo, turn that bass up and run that track back again. Rah, tell me he ain't murder that track."

Rah sat in the studio bobbing his head, smoking a blunt. listening to the young MC on the track. "Yeah, son fire. Who made the beat?"

"He made the beat and wrote the song in the same day."

"Yeah, yeah, I'm liking what I'm hearing, DJ."

DJ cut the music off and looked at Rah. "Rah, I know you been holding the streets down, doing what needs to be done. And the streets been talking about the episode on Avon. I'm just saying, Don Killer's block needs to be knocked off. He already caught you down bad before and he got a lot of dick riders in these streets. I'm staying ten toes down with you. You know my gun is your gun. I just want you to be on point out here."

"You know that's love, DJ, and I respect what you just said, but Don Killer ain't talking about shit. I just showed the streets that nigga ain't no God and he bleeds just like us."

"You damn sure did. I heard he was trying to get the fuck up out of there and his boy BG took a trip to the hospital, fighting for his life."

"Like I said, I showed the streets these niggas bleed. Now let me hear another track. I like son style of rapping."

***

"A-Dog, don't put the money in one bag. We are going to carry it on us. Look at how I got it on the inside of my coat." Murder showed A-Dog how he cut the inside of his Pelle Pelle and had a stack of $100 bills which came up to $75 grand lined up on the inside of his coat.

"I see what you doing, Murder. We going there to shop, but we are making it look like we are just there to talk at first."

"Big facts, now come on."

Murder looked at A-Dog as they pulled up to the spot. "You ready, dog?"

Both of them stepped out the car and walked into Omar's car and detail shop.

There was a white male standing at the counter with cut-off sleeves to his button down with tattoos all over his arms, who just looked at them when they walked inside. "What can I do for you two?"

"We came to see Omar."

The white male looked at them then passed them at the car they drove in. "Hold on, wait here." The white male came back a few seconds later. "Follow me." He led them through two doors that took them to the back of the shop.

That's when they saw Omar sitting on the hood of a car with one leg hanging off, talking on a cellphone. He hung up and walked over to them. "Do you know me? Because I don't know you, and anybody who comes here for me and ask by name must know me. So, as I look at you two and realize I don't know you, maybe you can tell me how you know me?"

Murder looked at Omar. "I don't know you, I know of you, but I was hoping I can get to know you."

"And why do you want to get to know me?"

"Because I had business I wanted to bring to the table."

"And what type of business can you bring to my table?"

Murder looked at A-Dog.

"I'll reach on the inside of my coat, if that's okay with you," replied A-Dog.

"It's not okay with me. Take the coat off and hand it to Pete, and he will get me whatever you are trying to get out. Is that okay with you?"

Murder and A-Dog took off their coats, handing them to Pete who picked them up and walked to the table, placing them there. He looked at Omar as he started to pull out stacks of money and placed them on the table.

"So you bring me money? Let me start this over. Who are you?"

"My name is Murder and this is my brother A-Dog."

"Okay, Mr. Murder, why did you bring me so much money?" asked Omar.

"Like I said when I first came in, I was hoping to do business with you."

Omar said something in Spanish to one of the other men in the back of the shop. Murder and A-Dog watched as he walked out the doors. "How much is this gift Pete put on my table, Mr. Murder?"

"A hundred and fifty thousand dollars."

"And what was you hoping to come out of that A hundred and fifty thousand dollars, Mr. Murder?"

Before Murder could say a word, the back door to the shop opened and Omar's man came driving Murder's car into the shop. Murder ain't say a word, he just looked at him. "Four car tires sir."

"Let me see your ID's, both of you, now."

Murder looked at A-Dog and walked over to Pete and handed him their IDs.

"Both of ya come back three hours from now. Let's say eight. The car is staying until you come back. Is that okay with you?" asked Omar.

"Yeah, it is."

"Good. Pete, show them out."

Once outside the shop, Pete handed them back their coats. "He said eight. Don't be late." He closed the shop doors as they walked off.

"Murder, what the fuck was that?" asked A-Dog.

"He's on a level we are trying to get on. Let's see what happens at eight when we come back."

"Yeah, let's see how this goes."

Chapter 22

"Nigga, stop walking, holding your chest like that shit hurt. Man, 2Pac said five shots couldn't drop him. He took it and smiled, so if that nigga could have five shots, it shouldn't be nothing to you."

"Fuck what you talking about, Don Killer. I felt the shell from that hot lead breaking up in my chest. That shit hurt."

"I know, man. I'm just fucking with you."

BG looked around the house. "Yo, where Monay at?"

"BG, I had to dismiss that bitch. She was talking sideways, talking about she got me this house and a bunch of other shit, talking about niggas showed me I wasn't bulletproof. I smacked the bitch out and poured a bottle on her. I'm glad that bitch kicked rocks."

"You sure that was the right move?" replied BG. "She been down from day one— picking up, dropping off, out of town trips and the plus was her people. People she plugged niggas on to."

"Fuck that bird. The plug knows where that bread and butter coming from and who got Amityville on lock. Fuck what they talking about. Omar don't want to lose our business."

"You right about that. So, what are we going to do about Rah?"

"I already got a team looking for him. You know we popping the bottle on him ASAP, homie."

"Copy that. Look, I'm tired as fuck so I'm about to close my eyes for the night, Don."

"I'm upstairs if you need me, bro."

"Cool."

***

"A-Dog, come on. It's that time."

Murder and A-Dog walked into the shop and were led to the back to where Omar was.

"I'm glad you made it on time. That's a good sign in my book, but I'm puzzled about you two. So, the only way I'll know the answer is if I ask the question. So, where ya'll operating at?"

"Amityville," replied Murder.

"What about Don Killer? Isn't that his turf?"

"With the upmost respect, Omar, fuck Don Killer. We hungry and we are going to eat."

"I like your attitude, Murder. Here's the deal. I'll give ya'll five car tires with the agreement I see ya every two months to get your tires rotated. Can you honor that?"

"Yeah, we can."

"Good. Your car's right there and everything is in the trunk you asked for with your IDs. I'll see ya two months from now on the fifteenth. If anything changes, come see Pete."

"We will."

Omar shook both of their hands before walking off.

***

Rah looked at his phone and saw he got a text message from Monay. He smiled to himself as he read the text. "*Hey, you. I was just texting you to see how your day was going. You ran across my mind. I know it's been over a week, but just know I was thinking of you. Take care. Monay.*"

Rah replied back to the message, "*What's up, beautiful? The right question is how have you been? I been busy lately, but I would like to see you if that's cool. If you ain't too busy sometime this week, let me know. Rah*"

Money replied, "*I'm free tomorrow around 2pm. How about we meet up at Red Lobster off of Sunrise Hwy and I'll have our table waiting for us.*"

"*Cool. I'll be there. Can't wait to see you,*" replied Rah.

Monay read the text and put her phone down. Her face was back to normal, and she was as beautiful as ever. She had a little house she was at right outside of Amityville in Deer Park she got a few years back to be her place of peace. Out of all the shit she and Don Killer had been through, he never put his hands on her. Besides the late nights, cheating, and staying out all night, he wasn't the type of man to bring her flowers and candy. He would give her $10,000 here, $15,000 there to go jewelry shopping. Most of the time she would put money up until she counted it one day and she had over $500,000 in cash. She saved up. It was 12AM so she started getting ready for bed. Rah wasn't going to be her new boo. She just enjoyed his conversation and she needed someone to talk to.

SAYNOMORE

Chapter 23

"Baby boy, how that chest feeling?"

BG was sitting at the table eating breakfast when Don Killer walked in the kitchen. "I'm straight, nigga. Stop acting like I was sounding like a bitch. I took that shit like a champ."

"I'm just messing with you, bro. You did that. Dead ass. Look, we got some pickups and drop-offs and I need to run by the barbershop. You up for a ride?"

"Hell yeah. Let me just get my hammer and we out," replied BG.

"Meet me in the car. I'm waiting on you."

BG got in the car and Don Killer look at him and laughed. "What's so funny, nigga?"

"Watching you walk with a cane like an old man. Look, we going to run by the two spots on Overland and Bayview. Cam said he had that paperwork ready for pickup and so did Drummer."

"How much work we got left?" asked BG.

"From the last pick up, about nine left. But like I told you before, we stretching it out as much as possible until this spick call me back."

"Yeah, Omar been getting beside himself lately, like he can't find himself six feet in a wooden box."

"His time is coming, but for right now, we just going to sit back and let him set himself up," replied Don.

"Don, who else is supposed to be here? You got cars in the driveway and in front of the house. This bitch is flooded."

"I don't know. Let's see what's going on."

Don Killer and BG walked through the house. They didn't anybody but heard noises coming from the basement. They looked at each other when they saw Drummer talking shit.

"The bet is a stack or better, side bets are three hundred-plus. We got Red Rum going up against Hitman with three rounds. Place your bets. Five minutes until the dogs hit the box." Drummer looked and saw Don Killer and BG in the corner of the basement. He walked over to them. "Don Killer, what's up, baby. BG, what it is, fam?"

"We are here to pick up. You got that ready for me?" asked Don Killer.

"Always, Don. Come upstairs. It's in the backroom."

Don Killer walked upstairs with BG behind Drummer to the backroom where he had a safe.

He pulled out $65,000 and handed it to Don Killer. "That's sixy-five large."

"I don't have to count this do I?" asked Don Killer.

"You know it's all there."

"I know." Don Killer patted Drummer on the back, opened his coat and handed him a kilo of cocaine. "I'll be back in two weeks. Here. Put three thousand on Hitman for me. That boy looks ready."

"Say less, Don. I'll call you and let you know if you won or not." Drummer watched as Don and BG walked up out.

"Let's go see what Cam got for us, BG."

***

Monay sat at the table drinking a glass of wine when Rah walked up to her. "Good afternoon, beautiful."

Monay smiled, got up and gave Rah a hug. "Hey. I see you made it. I went ahead and ordered for us. I hope you don't mind."

"No, I don't. So, what did you order us, Ms. Monay?"

"A lobster tail apiece and two seafood platters."

"Now that sounds good. And what are you drinking on?" asked Rah.

"I got us a bottle of champagne coming on ice, and don't worry, I paid for everything already," said Monay with a smile.

"Hold on, should I get on my hands and knees and ask the question, or wait until after we eat?"

Monay titled her head with a smirk. "Whatever Rahmelle."

"So, how is your day going, Monay?"

"It's good. I had a great morning. What about you?"

"It's cool. I'm really just getting out of my house. Coming to see you was the first thing I did today," replied Rah.

"You're handsome, well-dressed, white smile. Where's the female in your life, Rahmelle?"

"I could say the same thing about you. You are very beautiful, all the way laced, up and you don't mind paying for dinner. Who let you go?"

"You can't answer a question with a question, Rahmelle. I asked first."

"A lot of females don't know how to be themselves. It's always a hidden agenda they look for when they come up; what can they gain from a niggas. So, I keep it low, you feel me? It's no point to fake-kick it."

"I respect that. At least you keeping it real with them," replied Monay.

"So, what's your story now?" asked Rah.

"I've been with the same dude for nine years and he just couldn't control his sexual appetite. One female wasn't good enough for him after all I've done for him. We had a bad break up so I'm single now."

"Damn. I'm sorry to hear that."

Before Monay could say anything, the waiter came to the table with their food. They ate and talked for the next hour or so before leaving.

***

"How we looking, A-Dog?"

"Beautiful. I ain't going to lie, I ain't know what that guy Omar had in mind but he really player as fuck."

Murder stopped counting the money and walked over to A-Dog where he was weighing the coke. "I knew what time it was, that's why I told you to leave the guns here. He may have a cop or two working for him. He ran our names, background checks, check our car for a wire, shit like that. That's why I left the keys in the ignition. Shit smooth. Now we got a plug."

"Yeah, and we still got that issue with Don Killer," replied A-Dog.

"Yeah, I know. I been thinking about that since that issue on Avon. He been ducked off and I'm hearing he's been working off the phone and moved the trap houses."

"Yeah, I heard he got that nigga Pillz working out of one of them for him."

"I'll see what I can find out and we will go from there. Pillz is solid so we ain't going to fuck his wave up, but we might be able to use him to get to Don."

"And how is that?" asked A-Dog.

"Somebody got to pick up and drop the work off to him, and there goes our trail of breadcrumbs," said Murder.

"Hands down you right on that one. Look, everything weighed up. I'm about to pull up at Kim's spot. Tasha might be over there. What's up? take the ride with me?"

"Yeah, fuck it. Come on."

***

Don Killer sat at the red light talking with BG when he saw Monay's Lexus pass by, going up 110. He waited for the light to turn green and followed her.

"Don, I know you ain't on no stalking shit?" asked BG.

"Nah, I just want to see where this bitch been resting her head at. She knows way too much about what I got going on and I don't need her to be around the wrong niggas."

"I feel you on that one. I can't do nothing but respect that."

Don Killer just nodded as he followed her to a small white house in Deer Park. He rode past her as she pulled into the yard.

"So now you know where she at, now what?"

"Nothing. Let's get up out of here. I still need to go to the barbershop for the day is up."

Chapter 24

Monay was laying in her bed, asleep when her phone went off. She rolled over and saw it was Don Killer calling her. She dismissed the call and rolled back over. Before she could close her eyes, he was calling again. Monay grabbed the phone and cut it off. That's when her room door opened.

"Now that was disrespectful, Monay, to see me calling you and you just dismiss my call like that."

Monay jumped out of the bed. "How did you get in my house? How do you even know where I live?"

Don Killer picked up a picture Monay took years back at a nightclub and was looking at it. "I know everything, Monay. You must've forgot who the fuck I am. Get dressed. You coming with me back home."

"I am home and I ain't going no-fucking-where. And you need to get out, now."

Don Killer placed the picture back down and looked at Monay with a hard glare. "I said get dressed, you are coming with me, now. Don't fucking let me say it again, Monay."

"And I told you I'm not going no-fuckin-where with you. And I asked you to get the fuck out of my house."

Don Killer pulled his gun out off his waist.

"What, you going to shoot me now?"

"Naw, I'm not going to shoot you." Don Killer placed his gun on the dresser, walked up to Monay and went to give her a kiss.

She stepped back. "Don't touch me."

He smiled then back-slapped Monay so hard she fell backwards on the bed. "Now come here."

Monay tried to fight as she was kicking and trying to punch him. Don Killer punched Monay so hard in the forehead it took the fight out of her. He got on top of her and ripped her pants off as he had his hand wrapped around her throat, choking her. He pulled his pants down and forced himself inside of her. Monay let out a loud moan. He fucked her for 5 minutes as he looked at Monay with tears coming down her eyes.

After he came inside of her, he got up and pulled his pants up. "Now get dressed. I'm not going to ask you again. You try some dumb shit, I'll have someone pay a visit to your mother. Now try me if you want. Get dressed. Now." Don Killer walked out the room and into the kitchen as he waited for Monay.

She walked out the room a few minutes later with her head down and a bag over her shoulder.

"Now that's my girl. Come on." Don Killer picked up Monay's car keys and walked out of the house with her following him. Don Killer had one of his young soljas outside waiting for him. He looked at him and threw him Monay's car keys then nodded at him.

Monay got in Don Killer's car not saying another word as Don Killer got in and drove off. His young solja walked into Monay's house with a gallon of gas and poured it around everywhere. Then he walked to the front door, lit a match and set the house on fire before getting into Monay's car and driving off.

**

Monay walked into the house with Don Killer right behind her.

Don Killer stopped when he saw the headlights of Monay's car pulling into his driveway. He closed the front door. "Monay, put your things in the room and stay put until I get in there." Don Killer walked outside after he said that. "Is it done?"

"Yeah. Just like you said, the whole house is in flames. I poured gas in every room."

"Good, good. Let me get the keys and I'll see you tomorrow at the barbershop."

That young solja passed along the keys before walking back to his car.

Chapter 25

Monay couldn't sleep all night and when she did doze off it only felt like she was sleep for 5 minutes. She was sore between her legs to the touch. She got up and walked into the bathroom. She looked at her face where Don Killer punched her. There weren't any bruises there, but she did have some light bruises on her neck where he was chocking her. She walked back into the room, sat on the bed and turned her phone on. She had 5 missed calls and 4 voicemails from her next-door neighbor. She called her back after listening to her voicemails. "Hello, Jessie."

"Oh my God, Monay, I been trying to reach you all night. Your house caught on fire last night. It is totally destroyed. I'm sorry."

"Okay, I'm on my way there now, Jessica."

"I'm at work but call me when you get there."

"I will." Monay hung up the phone and got dressed. She picked up her car keys off the dresser and ran outside to her car and drove off. It took her 20 minutes to get there. When she pulled up you still saw smoke coming from the house. She got out of her car and walked inside the house, stepping over debris that was covering her small safe. She opened it to see that her money was unburnt. She put it all in the bag she was carrying and left the house. She put the bag in the trunk of her car and looked at her house one more time before driving off.

***

"Rah, what time is this man supposed to pull up?"

"He said by two, Rock. You know I just like to come by spots early to check out the layout, who inside and around. Look, I'm about to go to the bathroom. Order us two drinks."

"What you trying to drink on?" asked Rock.

"I don't know. Ciroc. Make it a double shot."

Rock ordered the drinks while Rah went to the bathroom. When he saw one of the pool tables was opened he walked to it so him and Rah could get a game going on when he came back.

"Now I know you ain't ready to see me on the table, Rock."

"I got hundred say that I am. So, what you talking about?" replied Rah.

"Rack them up, baby boy. I got time to kill."

***

Monay rode pass Jay's Sports Bar and saw Rah's car parked out front. She did a U-turn and pulled into the parking lot. She had a hood over her head and glasses covering her face. When she walked inside, she saw Rah playing pool with his boy. She took a seat behind a private booth with the little circular windows that you can see out of and still heard people talking. She didn't want to interrupt his game, so she was waiting until it was over to talk to him.

"Damn, shorty thick as fuck that just walked inside here, Rah."

Rah turned around and looked at the red bone go to the bar. "Yeah, she is fly. I like them hips."

"What's up with you and Don Killer bitch?" asked Rock.

Monay looked at Rock when he said that to Rah.

"She cool. She knows how to hold a conversation."

"So, you ain't fuck her yet?"

"We going to play pool or talk?"

"So, you ain't pipe her down yet? So, tell me this. Do she know you know who she is yet? That she Don Killer bitch?"

"No, she don't know I know, and I don't plan on telling her."

"Do she know who you are?"

"She knows my name is Rahmelle and that's all she needs to know."

"Rah, look. Ain't that our guy that just opened that back door?"

Rah looked and saw Neddy wave him and Rock back. "Yeah, come on."

Monay watched as they walked through the back door at the bar before she got up and walked out before they came back. She knew right then and there Rah was playing her from the jump. She promised herself she was going to show Rah and Don Killer who she really was and who they both fucked over.

***

"A-Dog, this is crazy. We eating. We got two traps popping, stacks on top of stacks. We really can go re-up right now."

"It's only been two weeks. We pulled a hundred and fifty-thousand already?"

"Naw, but we still have the money from the last shit we put up. I'll only have to take fifty-thousand out and we can put that back inside the stash when we make it back up," replied Murder.

"Shit, call him and see what he say then."

"Let me do that now then." Murder pulled out his phone and called Pete. After two rings he picked up. "Pete, it's Murder. I was seeing if I could make an appointment after tomorrow to get my tires rotated?"

"Hold on. Let me see if we have any openings tomorrow."

Murder waited until Pete came back on the phone quietly.

"Yeah, I see we have an opening tomorrow afternoon at five."

"Okay, that works just fine."

Pete hung up.

Murder walked back in the room where A-Dog was, "Everything good for tomorrow at five he said."

"Facts. You need me there? Because I'm trying to keep this trap running so we make money back and I don't want to miss out on not one penny, Murder."

"Shit, I'm good. I could go take care of it myself. I'm about to count this money up now. We on our way to the top with the house in the hills, dog," said Murder as he walked off.

***

Monay walked into the house and saw Don Killer sitting at the table. "You really burnt my fucking house down?"

"I don't know what you talking about, Monay."

"Yeah-fucking-right, Don. I can't fucking standing your trifling ass. I fucking hate you." Monay walked upstairs to the bedroom. She slammed the door. She went to open the nightstand so she could plug her phone up in the wall. That's when she saw Detective Joseph Watts' card in the drawer. She looked at the card one more time before closing the drawer. She sat on the bed and thought back to when the barbershop got shot up. She knew the name. She was just trying to put a face with it. She blew the thoughts out of her mind and went to take a shower.

Chapter 26

It was 5PM when Murder walked into the detail shop. Pete took him straight to the back to see Omar.

When they walked through the door, Omar was talking with one of his workers. He stopped when he saw Murder. "Murder, I thought I wouldn't see you for another five weeks. Things must be good on your end," said Omar as he walked up to Murder and shook his hand.

"Things are looking good on my end," replied Murder.

"Where your friend Dog at?"

"He ain't want to miss out on no money so he stayed behind this time."

"It don't take two people to do a one man job. I like that. So, the same thing as last time?"

"Yes." Murder began to take his coat off but Omar stopped him.

"You can hand Pete the money."

Murder did as he was told. "Do you want me to come back in a few hours?"

"No, you can wait around. Come have a seat and let's talk."

***

Monay walked downstairs and saw Don Killer and BG at the table.

"What's up, Monay?" said BG.

Monay just looked at him. "I'm going to get me somethings to wear because I don't have none here or no place else." Monay looked at Don Killer before walking out the door to her car. She pulled out the driveway and on her way to the mall, she ran over a pothole. "Fuck me! Shit." She pulled over and saw she bent her rim. "Fuck." She got into her car and drove to Omar's detail shop.

***

"Murder, I sat back and asked myself yesterday when Pete told me you wanted to come by again, how did you get rid of everything so fast? So, I thought of one of two things. One: the first time you came here, you ain't bring all your money? Or, two: you may be a cop, but I had a background check ran on you. So, I know you are not a cop. So, tell me, how are you moving things so fast?"

Murder looked at Omar. "The first time I came here I didn't bring all my money. All you gave me last time is gone but two tires."

That's when Pete walked into the office. "Omar, someone came by the shop I thought you might want to see."

Monay walked into the door. "Hey, hey, Omar!"

"Now look what the wind blew in. Come give me a hug, beautiful." Monay gave Omar a hug and kiss on the forehead. "So, tell me what brings you by today?"

"I bent my rim, Omar."

"That should be no problem to fix. I'm sure Pete is working on it now."

Monay looked at Murder.

"Monay, this is a new customer of mine. His name is Murder. Murder, this is Monay."

Murder got up and shook Monay's hand. "Nice to meet you."

"Likewise, Murder. So, where do you hustle?" asked Monay.

Murder looked at Monay then back at Omar. "Off of Smith Street by the junior high school."

"I know where that's at. It's in the cut. That's smart, but ain't that Don Killer turf?"

"I don't give a fuck about Don Killer. That's my block now."

Monay remembered Murder and the story of what happened to his friend and how Don Killer crossed both out after they showed him loyalty. Don Killer told her the story. "I'll let ya finish talking. It was good to see you, Omar, and nice meeting you, Murder. I hope I see you again."

"It was good seeing you tot, Monay. Now back to business. Murder, should I expect to see you again in two weeks?"

"No, the next time will be two months, Omar."

"Come. Pete waved to me, your car is ready. I'll see you in two months, Murder." Omar shook his hand.

"I'll see you soon, Omar." Murder got into his car and backed out the shop.

"What you think about him, Omar?"

"He's hungry, Pete, and a killer. His eyes tell a story of his past. He stands on loyalty. Come on. We have other business to deal with."

***

Monay walked into the house and Don Killer was talking with BG at the bar in the living room. As Monay was walking up the steps she overheard Don Killer telling BG, "I just got off the phone with Omar. He's going to be ready for us Friday. So, I need you to make the rounds and start to pick up everything. I need to know who's moving the most out they spot. We need to lock the block down again, and with this new shipment we are."

"How much we picking up?" asked BG.

"Thirty kilos," replied Don.

"What time?"

"Three."

Monay walked into their bedroom and closed the door.

Don Killer walked into the room a few minutes later to see Monay sitting on the bed reading a book. "Where you been all day?"

Without putting her book down or taking her eyes off of it, she replied, "The mall, then I went to get me something to eat."

"When I talk with you, give me the respect and look at me," replied Don Killer.

Monay placed the book down on the bed then looked at Don Killer. "The mall, then to get me something to eat."

"You been done since this morning and that's where you been all day?"

"Yeah. Now, if you don't mind, I would like to finish reading my book."

Don Killer looked at her and walked into the bathroom to take a shower. When he came out, Monay had the lights off in the room and was in the bed asleep. He looked at her and walked to the other side of the bed and laid down.

SAYNOMORE

Chapter 27

Murder walked into the trap to see A-Dog smoking a blunt watching Love and Hip Hop New York. "How we do last night, A-Dog?"

"We got off a few ounces."

Murder walked up to A-Dog and dapped him off.

"How the move go with Omar yesterday?" asked A-Dog.

"That shit went smooth. I picked up five. We still had two from the last run and three from the one before so we should be good. Nigga, pass the blunt and get ready so we can start weighing this work up."

"I been waiting on you, homie."

"Shit, come on then," replied Murder.

It was 2PM when A-Dog heard a knock at the door. He opened it and saw Monay standing there looking too good. "What's up, beautiful?"

"Is Murder here?" asked Monay.

"Yeah, come in. Murder, it's for you."

Murder walked out the kitchen to see Monay standing there in a black sweatsuit with black Nikes, and her hair pulled up in a ponytail. "Monay right?"

"Yeah, can we talk somewhere?"

"Yeah, come to the backroom. A-Dog, I'll be back in a minute."

"You good, homie," replied A-Dog.

Murder walked Monay to the backroom and closed the door. "What's good? How can I help you?"

"I was thinking maybe we can help each other out," replied Monay.

"And how is that?"

"I know you want to kill Don Killer for setting you and Trap up and killing your boy."

"How do you know about that?" asked Murder.

"I know a lot, Murder," replied Monay as she took a seat on the bed. "See, I'm not a killer but I will help you get to him."

"How I know I can trust you?"

"Omar trusts me just fine and you seen that yesterday."

"And what's in it for you?" asked Murder.

"You have to kill someone else for me and we split everything down the middle we get."

"Who do I have to kill?"

"Let's make sure we have a deal first and this is the only time I will bring this to the table. So, do we have a deal?" asked Monay.

"Yeah, we do."

"Good. I want Rah killed, and don't worry, I'll set both of them up for you. You just show up when I call."

"And when is all of this supposed to take place?"

"Friday before two."

Murder nodded.

"Where your phone at?"

Murder passed Monay his phone and watched as she put her phone number in to call herself.

"Be ready when I call you. I'll text you the address an hour before it's time."

"I'll be ready. Just make sure your shit is all the way lined up when you text me."

"It will be." Monay got up and walked out the bedroom with Murder behind her to the front door. "I'll be in touch, Murder."

Murder just nodded.

"Yo, who the fuck is she, Murder?" asked A-Dog.

"The key to killing Don Killer Friday."

"Can you trust her?"

"Omar trusts her and that's all that counts, so you ready?" asked Murder.

"Hands down you know I'm ready."

"Good, now let's finish up before it's too late."

***

Don Killer was in the barbershop playing pool, listening to Sports Center when BG walked inside. Don Killer laid the pool stick down and motioned for him to come to the backroom. Once behind the closed door BG took the bookbag off he was carrying. "How we looking out there?"

"Good but we could be doing better," replied BG.

"How much come in for the week?" asked Don Killer.

"Pillz had twelve thousand, Drummer had seventy-five thousand plus your six thousand on the dog fight, and Cam has twenty thousand. So altogether it was a total of a hundred and seven tousand. We been low the last few months. Our numbers was two hundred and fifty thousand every two to three weeks and that's with Rah and his team doing they thing on the other side of town, so that only tell me we got a trap opened somewhere that's not ours. "

"Yeah, and the only person who would tell us where it's at was killed a few weeks back with two one hundred dollar bills in his mouth, but we don't have time to worry about that. Omar just opened back the doors for us. So, this is what I need you to do. Meet me at the house tomorrow, let's say ten in the morning. We need to count all the money up and have the stash car ready. So, take all of this with you and just bring it by the house tomorrow," replied Don Killer.

"And what we going to do? Wait until we re-up before we go look for those little niggas again?"

"Yeah. I hate the fact that he still alive knowing we killed cops. That shit is getting under my skin every day I think about it."

"Yeah, just like the fact this dude Rah opened my chest up. Now he's playing hide and seek. I'ma unload the clip in his face when I get to him. Show him how to catch a body for real, for real."

"I'm about to get back to this pool game."

"Cool, we link up tomorrow before the move go down."

Don Killer dapped BG up before going back to the game.

***

Monay looked at her phone as she sat outside the Village drugstore. Rah texted her two times that she never replied back to. She laughed to herself as she stepped out of the car and walked into the store up to the counter.

"Good afternoon, how can I help you?" said the young man to her.

"Hello, I'm looking for something to help me sleep at night."

"Well, we have Tylenol PM and Advil PM. We also have Aleve too, that should help."

"No, handsome, I need something much stronger than that," said Monay.

"Anything stronger than that I'll need a prescription for."

Monay reached into her Gucci bag and pulled out $500, "I do have a prescription. Here you go."

The young man looked at the money then looked around. "Okay. Hold on, I'll be right back."

Monay waited until he came back as she checked the time on her phone.

"Hey, look, this is very strong. One pill will have you out for the whole day. So, I suggest you take a half a pill if you ain't trying to sleep all day."

"Okay. Thank you, handsome." Monay walked outside the drugstore, across the street to Radio Shack to pick up a few things before heading back home.

***

"Yo, Murder, I ain't going to lie. Baby girl that pulled up in here yesterday was tough as fuck. You ain't trying to get with that?"

"No, I'ma keep my hands out that cookie jar. Just because it look like honey don't mean it's sweet," replied Murder.

"Shit, I'll be Winnie da Pooh and taste that honey."

Murder just looked at A-Dog as he had his foot on the table smoking a blunt, talking shit.

"So, did she ever tell you why she was down to set this fool Don Killer up?" asked A-Dog.

"The only thing she said was she have her reason. But to be one hundred percent with you, we been trying to get at son. He just always have too many hittas around him. So, if she the way, I'll follow her lead. Plus, I told you the love that Omar gave her. He was talking business and everything in front of her, so I'm trusting his judgement, A-Dog."

"You know I'm rocking with you, so I'm down if you are down," replied A-Dog.

Gorillaz in the Trenches

"I already know my round."

SAYNOMORE

Chapter 28

Monay walked out the bathroom with just a thong on. Don Killer was sitting on the bed. He stood up, walked to her and wrapped his arms around her, placing kisses on the back of her neck. Monay looked at the clock on the wall. It was 9PM. She turned around and started to kiss Don Killer back passionately. He picked her up and carried her to the bed and laid her down as he started to kiss her stomach all the way down to her pearl. He opened her legs, kissing all over her thighs. As Monay had her hands on the top of Don Killer's head, she moaned lightly at the touch of his tongue on her clit as she moved her hips in a circle around his mouth. Don Killer stood up and pulled his boxers down, showing his thick 9-inch manhood. Monay sat up in the bed and leaned forward as she sucked on him. Don Killer let out a light moan when Monay started licking the head and neck of his manhood. She started to jack him off as she sucked on his sack. Don Killer stopped her as he pushed her back on the bed and placed himself inside of her. Monay dug her nails into his back as he started to pump in and out of her.

He stopped when he heard his phone going off. "Hold on, baby." He walked to the dresser and picked up the phone. "Yo, yo."

"I'm outside. You ready to count the rest of that money up?" asked BG.

Don Killer looked at Monay as she looked at him with a serious face. "Come to the door. I will be right down." Don Killer hung up.

"You can't be real right now, Don."

"I'm just going to give him this bag and I'll be right back." Don Killer opened the closet and grabbed the book bag out of it. He put his house robe on and met BG at the front door.

"Damn, Killer, you still in the bed?"

"Look, I'm good. It should be four in here. I counted it last night. Put the rest of what you got yesterday in there. Go pick up the stash car and be back here by noon so we can handle the business."

BG looked past Don Killer at Monay when she walked up behind him in a sexy red, small robe showing off her thick thighs.

"Don, you said you was coming right back," replied Monay.
Don Killer looked at her. "BG, text me when you done."

"Cool, I got it."

Don Killer closed the door and carried Monay back upstairs to the bedroom. Monay laid Don Killer down on his back as she got on top of him and started to ride him nice and slow as she kissed all over him. After 45 minutes of sex, Don Killer looked at Monay and kissed her forehead.

"Do you want something to drink, bae?" asked Monay.

"Yeah, let me get a double shot of Hennessey," replied Don Killer.

"Okay, I'll be right back, and when I come back I want a round two."

"You think you ready?" said Don Killer.

"Yeah, I am." Monay smiled as she walked out the room. She came back and handed Don Killer his drink and sat on the bed next to him as she took his shot. "How long are you going to be gone today?"

"I just have to take care of something with BG and I should be back home by five."

"Okay."

Don Killer got up to use the bathroom. When he came back in the room he sat on the bed as Monay kissed his neck right before he fell asleep. She looked at the time. It was 11AM. She grabbed his phone and texted Detective Joseph Watts. The text read, *"I can't talk, but here is the deal. I want all the heat off of me and my crew and I'll set you up with a bust of 30 kilos with Omar Knox at the shop today at 2PM. Reply back deal or no deal."* Monay sat the phone down and got dressed.

A few seconds later, BG was texting the phone. *"$500,000 on the head. I'm on my way to pick you up now."*

Monay replied back, *"Look, I need you to handle the business today with Omar. Everything's good. Text me back and let me know if it's too much for you or you can handle it?"*

"I got it man. I see you all boo'd up. I'll let you know how things went when I get back bro."

"Cool." Monay and picked up her phone and texted Murder. *"Be ready when I text you."* That's when she heard Don Killer's phone going off. She looked at the text message. *"Deal."* She replied back, *"Do you know where the shop is at?"*

"Yeah, I do."

"Good. Be on standby at 2pm. It's going down." Monay put the phone down and got dressed.

***

Omar hung up the phone and looked at Pete. "Have someone put Plick down and get everything out the shop now."

"I'm doing it now, sir."

***

It was 1PM when Don Killer opened his eyes. He could barely stand up he was so dizzy and he saw two of everything. He saw Monay standing in the room door. "Monay, what the fuck did you do to me?"

Monay texted Murder with the address and told him to come now, the front door was opened. "Nothing yet," replied Monay.

"Bitch, I will kill you."

"I know you will, but what will happen if you die first?"

Don Killer went to rush Monay but was too dizzy. Monay moved out the way as Don Killer fell down the steps to the living room floor. Monay walked down the stairs and was looking at Don Killer on the floor laying on his back. Monay walked up to him and kicked him in the stomach. When he rolled over, she took the tape she had on the table and taped his hands and feet up.

"Do you really think you going to get away with this? BG on his way over here right now."

"Don," said Monay. "BG's not coming. He should be already dead."

"So why ain't I dead yet?"

"Don't worry. Somebody is coming to see you right now."

"So, you think you are that smart?" replied Don Killer.

"I am, Don. Let me tell you how you set yourself and friend up to be killed. About two weeks ago I saw you had Detective Joseph Watts' card in the nightstand. I knew the name but I couldn't put a face with it. Then it came to me, dodo, I met him before at Omar's detail shop. Omar introduced me to him as someone who works for him but my plan ain't come together until I heard you and BG talking about the big pickup Friday at two. I knew when I bent my rim and I went by the shop you would never guess who Omar had there Murder. And I remember the story you told me how you killed his boy Trap. So, I let him talk and found out where he was at then I made a deal with him to come here today to kill you. But I needed you and BG to be separated from each other. So, I fucked you so you would be open to trust me. Then, when I got you your drink, I drugged you and I texted Detective Joseph Watts from your phone about the deal that was going down today, knowing he was going to let Omar know you was trying to set him up. Then I texted BG and played with his pride from your phone and asked him can he handle the deal without you. If it's too big of a deal, you'd come. Of course, his pride got in the way and he said he can handle it. And now here you are, tied up on the floor about to die. The big, bad Don Killer. Thought he had it all figured out. You treated me like I was a dog in the streets, poured E & J all over me and you raped and beat me. Then you set my house on fire. You thought you was going to walk away from that? I fucking hate you and I can't wait to look at your lifeless body."

Don Killer just laid on the floor in disbelief at everything Monay just told him. That's when he heard the front door open. He turned his head to see two men walk in the house, guns, out with masks over their faces. Monay stood up and walked to them. Murder pulled his mask off.

Monay looked at him. "He's all yours, Murder, as promised. I'll be in the next room."

Murder nodded at Monay as she walked out the living room.

***

BG pulled the car to the back of the shop doors. He waited as the doors opened. Pete waved for him to pull in. Once inside, Pete closed the doors and Omar stepped out of the car.

"BG, where is Don at? I was hoping to see him."

"He had some other business to attend to, but he trusted me to handle this today."

"I see. See, that's where the problem comes in at. I got a phone call today from a Detective friend of mine who knew about this meeting today and all that was to take place. And the only people who knew about this meeting was you, Don, me and Pete. So how do the cops know about it? And why is Don not here? So, now I see he tried to set me up."

"Omar, I don't know nothing about that. Let me call Don Killer to see what's going on real quick," replied BG nervously.

"Go ahead. I will wait."

BG pulled his phone out and called Don Killer but he never answered the phone. He tried two times. "Omar, I don't know why he ain't picking up the phone."

"Don't worry about it, BG." Omar nodded to Pete.

Pete smacked BG in the back of the head with a crowbar, knocking him out cold.

"Kill him, chop his body up and dump him in the trash somewhere and get rid of the car." Omar walked off after saying that to Pete.

***

"Look at you, Don Killer, all the fucked up. Shit you did came back on you, now look at you."

"Fuck you, nigga. I ain't about to go out weak pussy."

"I don't want you to go out weak. Just know when we killed Trance that night and them cops, me and Trap stood next to you on loyalty. Then you crossed us out and set us up to be killed. You killed my brother," said Murder as his trigger finger itched.

"Fuck him," replied Don Killer.

"No, fuck you." Murder put the gun to Don Killer's head and pulled the trigger 3 times, killing him. He then shot him two more times in the chest.

Monay came out the other room a few minutes later with a roll of trash bags in her hands. "I don't move dead bodies, and under the counter where the sink is at is a gallon of bleach and pine scent."

Murder just looked at her and took the bags out of her hand and went to work.

Chapter 29

Rah walked into the basement and saw Rock cooking up the coke as he watched the New York Giants game on TV. "How we looking down here, Rock?"

"Smooth. I'm almost done. You trying to cook up five kilos. I already cooked up three of them."

"No, after you finish what you have, we are going to pause for a minute until we get that up off us."

"So, who you think killed that boy Don Killer and BG?" asked Rock.

"I don't know, but they had that shit coming," replied Rah.

"They said BG's body was in different parts of Amityville, in the back of store dumpsters. They made a point out of that boy. You talk to his bitch lately?"

"We had a few phone conversations and some text messages back and forth, but that shit is getting dried up."

"No word on who working that side of town yet?" asked Rock.

"I don't know, but I do know they still moving a lot of weight over there, so Don Killer getting bodied ain't slow shit down." Rah opened the refrigerator, pulled out a grape soda, walked to the table and started to roll up a blunt.

"You don't think Monay might know what really happened? The real story behind they deaths?"

"To tell you the truth, I don't give two fucks about it, hands down. Now I came to watch the game, not talk about a dead man."

"Shit, I don't know why we all know how the game going to end, with a loss to the Giants."

"There you go hating already," replied Rah.

"Facts are facts."

"Are you done?"

"Yeah."

"Good." Rah turned the TV up as he watched the game.

***

Murder walked into the cemetery up to Trap's gravesite. He kneeled and placed his hand on top of Trap's headstone. "What's up, little bro? I know it's been a while since I been here, but it's hard without you, family. But I came to let you know I got that nigga. I put three in his head and two in his chest. I know it took a minute, but I wasn't going to let that shit ride. I'm fucking with A-Dog out here making the money and we got a good plug. Your peoples is good too. I gave your mother your cut on what I got from out of Don Killer's spots. It was twenty birds, but I only gave her two hundred thousand. I had to break bread with A-Dog, but on the gang, I'ma hold her down until I stop breathing, homie." Murder had a tear come down his eyes as he talked to Trap. "Look, I got to go. Stay watching over me, bro. I love you, my nigga." Murder got up and walked away with his head down. That's when his phone started to ring. He saw it was Pete calling him. He stopped and picked up the phone. "Hello."

"Hey, I'm calling from Omar's Detail Shop. I just wanted to let you know that your car parts came in today and we have an opening today at four. Do you think you can make that appointment?"

"Sure, I can be there, and thank you for the call," replied Murder.

"You're welcome, and we look forward to seeing you then."

Murder hung up the phone and looked at the time. It was 2:45PM. He then called A-Dog.

After two rings he picked up. "What's good, Murder?"

"Clean everything up. I need you to take a ride with me to the detail shop. They just called me, and the car parts just came in. I'm on my way now to get you."

"I'll be ready when you get here, fam."

"Copy that." Murder hung up, got into his car and drove off to pick up A-Dog.

***

"Murder, did you order some more work?" asked A-Dog.

"No, Pete called me out the blue. I don't know what this is about."

"Real shit. I hate not knowing and we are going in there without our heat. This shit don't feel right."

120

"We good. Come on, let's see what this is about."

Pete met Murder and A-Dog at the door and waved to them to follow him to the back of the shop.

That's when they saw Omar standing there, smoking a cigar. "Murder, I'm glad you made it. Come in my office. We need to talk. A-Dog, it's good to see you, too."

"Likewise, Omar," replied A-Dog.

As they walked into the office, Omar sat behind his desk. "Please, take a seat, the two of you. So, I guess you are wondering why I called you here?"

"You took the words right out my mouth," said Murder.

"Here's the thing. Don Killer is dead and so is BG. Both of them were pieces of shit if you ask me, but here is the big picture. From Sunrise Highway up Greatneck Road to 110 and the little side blocks he had, I need someone to take over. Yesterday I could look in your eyes and tell you are hungry, Murder. Do you think you can handle ten to fifteen kilos a month and take over Don Killer's blocks?"

"Fifteen kilos is a lot of work. I'm not saying I can't do it, but I need to make sure I can deliver on my end. Because when you want your money, you are not going to want to hear tomorrow or next week. So, let me do my networking first before I can agree to anything?" replied Murder.

"I respect your honesty. Murder, let's say Friday you will let me know something?"

"I can do that Friday by four at the latest."

"I hope next time I see you it will be a slow yes rather than a four-day wait to hear you say no," replied Omar.

Murder didn't say nothing. He got up and shook Omar's hand. "I'll see you Friday, sir."

"Yes, you will."

After walking outside back to the, car A-Dog looked at Murder. "We could do that shit, Murder, and run all of this shit."

"A-Dog, we are talking fifteen kilos a month, thirty-thousand a brick. That's four hundred and fifty-thousand dollars a month. It's going to take more than just us two. And then you still have Don

Killer people on the block, so we have to put the murder game down. Omar wants an answer in four days. That means the trap stops and we got to go do this leg work starting now."

"Fuck it. Let's go."

"Say less. We are headed to Overland now."

***

Murder pulled in the driveway and looked at A-Dog before getting out the car. "Come on. Let's do this." Murder knocked on the door twice.

When the door opened, he was looking at Cam. "What's up? I don't do walk-ins. Call the jack and then pull up."

"I just came to talk to you about some business, Cam, then we on our way."

Cam looked at Murder and A-Dog. "Come in and make it worth my time."

When Murder looked inside, he saw Cam had someone there with him, smoking a blunt.

"So, what type of business you want to talk about, nigga?" asked Cam.

"I'll jump to the point," replied Murder.

"Yeah, do so."

"Don Killer's dead and so is BG. I can supply you with whatever you need. Bricks going for thirty-seven a kilo."

Cam looked at his homie smoking the blunt then back at Murder. "So now that Don Killer's dead you think you can call roll in his spot and tell me what you can do for me? It sounds to me like you trying to take this shit over. What make you think I need you, nigga?"

"Fuck this shit," said A-Dog as he pulled his gun out and shot Cam dead in the face, clapping him.

Murder pulled his gun out on his home boy. "You trying to get this paper, or you want to take a ride with this nigga? Talk fast."

"Trying to get this paper."

"Smart choice. What you holding in the house right now?" asked Murder.

"Shit, we down to the last two ounces. It ain't been no work since Don Killer been dead."

"How much ya pull out of here a month?"

"Maybe forty if the work is here."

"This is my trap now, but you are going to work it. I'll start you off with one kilo for thirty-seven on Friday. I have no problem with killing a nigga so don't try me."

"I'm just trying to eat."

"Good, now help Dog put this nigga in the trunk of the car. I got some other stops I need to make."

A-Dog looked at Murder and smiled once in the car. "Where we headed now?"

"To go see Pillz on Bayview. I hope he got more of an understanding than the nigga in the trunk."

"If not, we got room back there for another body, Murder."

"Let's go see Pillz, A-Dog."

***

"Pillz, we go back to the sandbox. You stand up and solid, hands down. So, it's only right we eat together," replied Murder.

"You right. We do go back to the sandbox and basement parties. I fucks with you, Murder, so tell me what ya got in mind?"

"Don Killer is dead, the block is drying up, and niggas are going to start losing customers and you don't need that," said Murder.

"So, what you have in mind," asked Pillz curiously, "and don't forgot you got Cam around the block trying to step in Killer's place. He already pulled up on me about the numbers at this spot."

A-Dog smiled when he heard Pillz say that.

"Don't worry about Cam. He's taken care of already, and I'll supply you with the work starting with a kilo for thirty-seven-thousand. How that sound?" asked Murder.

"That shit sound sweet. Don Killer was charging forty-two a bird, but what you mean you took care of Cam already, because I know that nigga going to be a problem."

"Pillz, let me show you something real quick. Walk with me to the car. I got something in the trunk I need to show you."

Pillz walked to the trunk of the car with Murder. He watched as Murder popped the trunk. "Oh shit." Pillz looked at Murder.

"Like I said, I took care of Cam. He ain't want to rock wit us so rock-a-bye, baby."

Pillz looked at Cam's dead body one more time then back at Murder.

"I'll see you Friday with the brick."

"Cool I'll be here."

Murder dapped Pillz up one more time before getting in the car driving off.

"That's two traps plus ours. Both of them said they can pull the thirty-seven thousand within a month. That's seventy-four from them. We pulling in a hundred-fifty so we still need to make up a hundred and seventy-six."

"We need workers on the block, Murder," replied A-Dog.

"No, that's hot. We need the barbershop on 110. I need to call Monay and try to meet up with her today, but first we need to dump this body on the side of the road somewhere."

Chapter 30

Monay waited patiently for Murder in the abandoned parking lot. She watched as he pulled up in an all-black Dodge charger. He stepped out of his car and into her white G-Wagon. "This shit is nice, Monay," said Murder.

"Thanks. So, what's up? What you need to talk to me about?" asked Monay.

"Our friend Omar wants me to take over Don Killer's turf. I'm cool with that, but I need the shop."

"You know Scooby got the shop right now."

"But he don't have no work to run it and soon his customers are going to go to Rah and his team."

"You might have a point. So, what you putting on the table?"

"I got the bricks for thirty-seven a pop. Have him shop with me from now on and we all can eat."

"And what's in it for me?" asked Monay.

"What you want?"

"Thirty-seven percent from the barbershop off the top every month on what you pull in."

"As long as I got your agreement I'm the only one who will be supplying the shop."

"You have my word."

"Then it's a deal."

"Don't forget about what you still owe me, Murder."

"I'm just waiting on your call, Monay." Murder opened the door and walked back to his car as he watched Monay drive off.

***

"Murder, how it go with Monay?"

"Good. She wants thirty percent from the barbershop, but I knew that was going to come with a price."

"So, we good. We covered all bases. So, getting off the work shouldn't be a problem."

"No, it shouldn't be but I'm not going to put that much pressure on our shoulders. So, I'll tell him we good and we can move the work but the timetable will be two months, not one. That's the only way just in case something don't work out, we got time to fix it," replied Murder.

"So, when you want to pull up on him?"

"I'm going to wait until Friday and I'm willing to bet he will have everything there when we get there. He's that sure of himself."

"It's on then. You the head nigga now in these streets."

"Come on. Let's figure out how we going to do these drops."

***

Rah looked at Monay and smiled. "It's been a minute. I thought you dropped me."

"No, I just had a lot on my plate I had to take care of. My mind was everywhere, but how you been?"

"I have been good, staying focused. You know, just having a positive vibe." Rah looked out the diner window at Monay's white on white G-Wagon. "So, you put the Lexus to the side and came out in the G-Wagon. That's how you living, Monay?"

"No, I'm just on my hot girl shit right now. I'm trying to get up there with you, Rahmelle. Rocking the diamond encrusted Rolex, diamond earrings. You up-up. This lunch is on you, right?"

Rah started to laugh as he took a sip of his drink. "Yeah, it's on me today, beautiful. So, if you don't mind me asking, how you get your paper?"

"Let's just say I know how to make smart investments and how to stay clean. What about you? Wait, I forgot you told me you was a dope boy."

"You make it sounds like I'm a killer, the bad guy," re-plied Rah.

"It's levels to the dope game depending on what level you are on. Sometime a body is necessary or two." Monay smiled as she took her sip of wine, looking Rah in the eyes.

"Have you ever killed anybody, Monay?"

Monay looked Rah dead in the eyes. "I have ordered the death of people and watched as they were killed. What about you, Rah? Do you have blood on your hands?"

126

"I never ordered the hit on nobody. I got up close on them and killed them myself. Headshot."

"I guess," replied Monay.

"That don't frighten you, Monay?"

"I been around killers. I lived with them. I'm not scared of a man with a gun. I'm scared to be caught without mine, Rahmelle."

"I guess there's more to you than a pretty face, Monay, and a beautiful body. When can I meet the woman behind the pretty face?" asked Rah.

"You already met her. She just knows how to show two faces at one time."

"So, let's talk money then. Let's say I can get you a kilo for forty-three thousand a pop. How does that sound?"

"It sounds fair, but what if I tell you I have a friend who can get them at thirty-seven a pop? It's ninety-seven to ninety-eight percent pure."

Rah looked at Monay to see if she was bluffing. "If you can get them at thirty-seven, what if I told you I want two this week. Can you get them?"

"Yeah, and just know business is a different conversation and every dollar needs to be accounted for."

"Let's do this Friday then, Monay."

"It's going to be on my terms, my location and you can bring one person with you. And when we do our business they stay out of our conversation. Do I make myself clear?"

"Yeah, and I guess this is the other face," replied Rah.

"Like I said. I can show two faces at one time, Rahmelle."

Rah and Monay talked for the next hour before he walked her to her truck and watched her pull off.

***

Rah picked up the phone and called Rock.

He picked up after a few rings. "Yo, Rah, what the word, lover boy?"

"I just left Monay. She just told me she got them for thirty-seven. I ordered two for Friday."

"So, what? This bitch trying to jump in Don Killer shoes now and become the dope queen?"

"I don't know, I'm still trying to figure her out. She pulled up in the new G-Wagon. Her conversation was different. Even her vibe," said Rah.

"She might have found that nigga stash. You know he was up-up on the bread and the work, and now she driving a G-Wagon. I wouldn't put it past her," said Rock.

"Yeah, she said it was a friend of hers, but I think she was talking about herself in the third person."

"Let's kidnap the bitch, tie her up and see what she got."

"I'm about to pull up on you. We ain't talking no more over the phone."

"I'm at the white house."

"Copy that."

Chapter 31

Murder walked into the detail shop through the backdoors. He stopped when he saw Omar talking with someone. Omar looked at him and gestured for him to hold up for one second. As he looked around, he saw Omar walking toward him.

"Murder, I see you made it. Come in my office. Let's talk."

"A man stands on his word and I stands on mine, Mr. Omar. I can do what you asked me but in sixty days, not in thirty. Let me get my clientele and movement up, and then down the line we can talk about the length of time and narrow it down to what you are asking me for."

"Again, Murder, I like your honesty. We will do the sixty days on your terms, but I have one of my own. Twenty kilos every sixty days."

"And what's your numbers on each kilo?" asked Murder.

"I'll do twenty-five thousand a kilo for the first year. Then, I want thirty thousand. That should give you enough time to get everything situated. Agreed?" replied Omar.

Murder reached his hand over Omar's desk to shake his hand. "Agreed. When can I get my first shipment?"

Omar lit his cigar and looked at Murder. "It's already in the trunk of the car."

"Of course, it is." Murder laughed. "I'll see you in sixty days, Omar."

"Murder, that's five hundred thousand dollars when I see you next time."

Murder nodded and walked off. Murder got a text from Monay that said, *"I need 2 and you can meet me at the same spot we talked at last time by 6pm. I'll be waiting."*

Murder replied, *"I'll be there."*

***

Murder pulled up to the trap where A-Dog was waiting on him. He pulled into the back of the house. A-Dog opened the door for him.

"Look, help me get these bags inside. We already running late, and I have to meet Monay at six with two birds. I need you to take Pillz and Cal they birds apiece. You cool with that?" Murder asked.

"You know I got that in the bag already." A-Dog put the bag on the table and looked at Murder. "How many he gave us?"

"Twenty for five hundred. We got sixty days to get this money up." Murder spoke.

Murder took four kilos out of the bag. He took both bags and put in the sage before hiding it in the closet.

"I'm about to handle this business with Monay. Hit me up when you get done dropping off the work."

"Cool. I'm out, Murder. I'll hit your line when I'm done."

Murder dapped A-Dog up before walking off with the bag of bricks.

***

A-Dog put the bookbag in the backseat of his BMW. He got in the car and put Meek Mill on before driving off. The song was Who You Around featuring Mary J. Blige It took him twenty minutes to get to Cal's spot on Overland. He pulled over in front of the house. He checked his gun to make sure he had a full clip before getting out. He took the bookbag out of the car and walked in the house. Cal was there smoking a blunt, weighing a few grams up.

"What's good homie? You ready to rock and roll and get this bread?"

"Shit, I been waiting on you all day," replied Cal.

"Let me show you what I got." A-Dog put the kilo on the table and cut it open in the middle then smiled at Cal. "This that real deal, nigga. Ninety-seven percent pure. It's going to have them baseheads jumping gates to get to you."

"Yeah, that's that butter right there. I can tell."

"Look, I got another drop to make, I'll see you in thirty days with that thirty-seven. If you get this off before then hit me up and I'll pull up with another bird."

"Say less."

A-Dog grabbed the bookbag, walked back to his car and drove off

***

Murder walked up to Monay's truck and got in. He placed the bookbag on the floor between his legs.

"What's up, Monay?"

"Nothing, I need you to take a ride with me. This dude Rah wants two kilos. I told him thirty-seven apiece."

"He's supposed to meet me in the village under the tracks at seven-thirty."

"So, you want me to pull up on him?" asked Murder.

"No, I'll do the talking. I just need you to watch my back to make sure shit goes right."

"Cool, I got you. We driving this?"

"No." Monay pointed to a black-on-black Chrysler 300.

"Come on. I don't want to be late."

When they pulled up to the tracks, Rah was already there leaning against the front of his car with Rock. Monay got out and stepped in the front of the Chrysler. Murder got out of the other car with the bookbag in his hand.

"Wait here. Let me see what he talking about," Monay coached.

"Don't worry. I got you and I'm watching everything," replied Murder.

Monay started to walk up to Rah. He met her halfway.

"Damn, you look beautiful, sexy," Rah said as he licked his lips.

"I told you when it's business, it's a different conversation. Where's the money?" Monay asked.

Rah looked at her then pass her at Murder. "It's in the car."

"Shouldn't it be with you?"

Rah turned his head and waved Rock over with the money.

"Tell your boy to stop."

"Hold up, Rock. What's up, Monay?"

"I told you when we do business, it's me and you. No one in our conversation. You can go get the money and come back. I don't need him in our business. I'll be right here."

"You know what? I forgot you said that. That's cool. Hold up."

Monay watched Rah as he walked off.

"What's up with shorty? She doing too much." replied Rock.

"Just chill. I got this." Rah took the bag and walked up to Monay. "Seventy-four thousand in cash. Hundreds, fifties and twenties."

He handed Monay the bag. Monay looked inside it.

"I'll be back in a minute." She walked off to the car and got inside and put the money in a portable counter. She stepped out the car three minutes later and took the bag from Murder. She walked back up to Rah and handed him the bag.

"There are two birds in there. Ninety-seven percent pure. I'll wait here while you go check it out." replied Monay.

Rah looked inside the bookbag, nodded then walked off. "Rock make sure this is what she said it is."

Rock got in the car and took his knife out. He opened the middle of the brick, dug his knife inside and sniffed a line of it. He looked at Rah and gave him the thumbs up. Rah walked back to Monay.

"I appreciate that business, Monay."

"Likewise, Rahmelle. Take care."

Monay turned around and walked off. Rah just watched her as she got into the car and drove off. He walked back to his car.

"You good bro?" Rock asked.

"Yeah, I think we found out who killed Don Killer and put the crown on her head." Rah spoke.

"You think so?"

"There's no doubt in my mind. She just showed me she a cold bitch."

"So, you still going to shop with her?"

"Until we knock her block off and take what she got. We just got to sleepwalk her right now until the ball is in our court. Let's get the fuck up out of here."

***

"Playboy, what's up? You ready to get this baby love?" asked A-Dog.

"Waiting on you." said Pill.

"Well, the wait is over. Let's step inside."

Pillz walked A-Dog inside to the kitchen.

"Check it out. Ninety-seven percent pure. This shit is better than pussy, baby boy."

"Yeah, yeah, that's that guy," replied Pillz.

"You can cut this three times and still make your money."

"I'm out. Hit me when you ready for another bird. You know the ticket already. Thirty-seven bands."

"That's no pressure. I'll hit you as soon as I get this off."

A-Dog nodded as he walked out the door, closing it behind him.

***

"It's seventy-four thousand in that bag, Murder. Tomorrow I'm supposed to meet with Scooby. I'll call and let you know where to meet me at with the kilos." said Monay.

"Cool, I'll be waiting for your call."

Murder got out the Chrysler and walked to his car. Monay watched as he drove off. She parked the 300 back where it was, got into her G-Wagon and drove off.

SAYNOMORE

Chapter 32

Rah watched as Rock weighed up the bricks and was testing the presence of it.

"How we looking, Rock?"

"This shit is A one. We can cut this two maybe three times and won't take no losses," replied Rock. "Let me find out she always been the plug."

"No, she ain't. She the middleman. And whoever she was with was her shooter."

"Rah, you told me she had a G-Wagon. I remember the black Lexus from the night at the club. Now, she pulled up in the big body, black on black 300. She popping her shit. If she ain't the plug, she found Don Killer's stash."

"We need to find out who she know and who she plugged in with because last night I didn't even know the bitch I was talking to." said Rah.

"Nigga I do. A boss bitch."

Rah pulled out a Newport and lit it.

"I'll see if I can link up with her this week and see what I can get out of her."

"You might need to put someone else on to her so she don't try and put two and two together before we can hit the lick."

"Let me think about that. I'm about to make a move. Let me know when that shit is cooked up."

"I'll hit your line when I'm done," said Rock.

"Do that."

***

Monay pulled up to the barbershop in her G-Wagon. She stepped out looking like a true dime piece, someone who should be on a Covergirl poster. When she walked into the barbershop, all eyes were on her as she stopped at the door and took her glasses off. Scooby smiled when he saw her.

"Monay, I see you, beautiful."

"I see you too, Scooby. Come on, let's go talk in the backroom."

Scooby followed Monay to the backroom and closed the door when he stepped inside.

"I take it you ready for me, Monay," said Scooby.

"I am and I'm also here for the money from the last drop that you got from Don Killer."

"What do that got to do with what we got going on now?" asked Scooby.

"What? You think because Don Killer is dead old business goes away? No boo boo, it don't work like that. Just another nigga takes his spot and the money still get rotated. So, I'm waiting, Scooby."

"I respect that, Monay."

Scooby walked to the safe, opened it up and handed Monay $86,000.

"That's eighty-six right there."

"Thank you. I'll be back later with 2 birds for you and the price just went down to thirty-seven a brick. That work for you?"

"I have no complaints. Monay, you a tough bitch. I like your style."

"I'll be back in a few hours with your package."

Monay put the money in her bag and walked off.

***

"How that shit go last night with Monay you never told me, Murder?" A-Dog asked.

"She played her part hands down. Now, I know why Don Killer kept her around. All the money was accounted for. I just can't figure out her angle right now."

"You think she trying to work one over on you?"

"No, but it's funny how she helped us body Don Killer and how she want us to kill Rah. But she just did a seventy-four-thousand-dollar drug deal with him on two bricks. Shit just don't add up to me," replied Murder.

"You said you can trust her because of Omar so fuck it. Don't put too much thought into that shit."

"Yeah, I guess you right. I just know how the streets work and how the streets have no love for no one."

"Shit, the streets is showing us mad love. Just look on the counter. We got bricks on bricks. That's over two hundred thousand right there and we getting the bricks for the low low. I say that's love, Murder,"

"Yo, hold up dog. This Monay calling me. Monay, what's up?"

"You at the same spot I came and saw you at before?" asked Monay.

"Yeah, but I'm about to make a run to take care of something. I should be back in about an hour," replied Murder.

"Okay, I'll come see you in an hour and a half. I have something for you."

"See you in a few."

Murder hung up the phone and walked back over to A-Dog.

"Monay will be here in an hour or so. I want to take 10 of them kilos and the money to the other spot. We got too much money and kilos in here right now. It's not a good look. Anything can go wrong, feel me?"

"You making a good point. You trying to do that now?" replied A-Dog.

"Yeah"

"Let me go get the bags out the back for you. I'll be right back."

A-Dog walked back in the kitchen and put the black bag on the table. He placed eleven bricks inside with the money.

"Murder, I put 11 bricks inside with the money. How long you going to be gone?"

"I'll be back within an hour." Murder pulled up the bag and walked out the house. Once in the car, he drove around Amityville until he pulled up at the other spot. He put everything up and was on his way back to A-Dog.

***

A-Dog was smoking a blunt watching Kevin Hart's *Laugh at my Pain* when Pillz called him. He looked at the phone as it was going off.

"You done so soon, baby boy?" A-Dog asked.

"The way shit is moving I will be by the end of the week. You heard from Cal?" asked Pillz. "Because all his people are buying from me. I called his jack a few times, but he ain't been picking up."

A-Dog put the blunt down in the ashtray and cut the TV off.

"Pillz, say that again?"

"He ain't picking up his line."

"Yo, let me call you right back."

A-Dog hung up the phone and called Cal but he ain't pick up. When he tried it again, it went right to voicemail.

"This nigga want to fucking die playing with my shit."

A-Dog picked up his gun off the table, locked the house up and got in his car and drove to Overland Ave. He pulled up in front of Cal spot. He got out looked around and walked into the house. Nobody was there everything was gone. The T.V., furniture, dogs. That's when he saw that Cal played him and Murder. He took off with they shit. He took out his phone and called Murder.

"Yo, I'm on my way back now, fam." Murder said.

"Man, we got a bigger problem than that, Murder," replied A-Dog.

"What you talking about?"

"This nigga Cal ran off with our shit. I'm over here on Overland now. The spot is empty all the way."

"Post up. I'm on my way over there now, homie."

"Say less. I'll see you when you get here."

A-Dog hung the phone up and walked around the house in every room, gun is his hand. He walked to the front door when he heard Murder's car pulled up. He opened the front door and waited for him to come inside. Murder walked into the empty house.

"This nigga really played his fucking self. He moved. You tried calling him?" asked Murder.

"Yeah, a few times within the last 45 minutes."

"Let me try calling him real quick."

Murder called his phone, but it was disconnected.

"Yo dog, is this the number you got for this nigga?" Murder showed A-Dog the number.

"Yeah, that's it. That's the same number I got."

"I just called it and it said it was disconnected."

"Let me try from my jack."

Murder looked at A-Dog's facial expression and knew that he disconnected his line.

"Yo, I'll kill this motherfucker on the gang."

"Come on, I got to meet Monay. We will deal with this shit later."

"I'ma put a ticket on his head. How much you think?"

"Five thousand dollars," said Murder.

"Copy."

***

Monay pulled up to the trap house as Murder and A-Dog was coming down the street in their cars.

She looked at both of them as they pulled up and got out of the cars.

"You just got here, Monay?" asked Murder.

"Yeah, a few seconds ago. Come on, let's go inside."

Monay looked at A-Dog's expression and knew something was wrong.

"A-Dog, right?"

"Yeah, how are you doing Monay? I got a lot of my mind. My bad for not speaking."

"It's cool."

Monay walked into the house behind Murder. Once the front door was closed, she looked at both of them.

"What's up? What happened?"

Murder looked at her. "One of the guys ran off with some work."

"How much?" asked Monay.

"A brick."

"Who was it?"

"A nigga named Cal who was trapping off Overland," said Murder.

"I hate fuck niggas. He's going to turn up," replied Monay.

"And when he does, he's a dead man."

"And make sure you keep that promise to death Murder. Now, I got something for you."

"And what's that?" asked Murder.

"Seventy-four thousand dollars. I need two and I need you to take a ride with me if you are not busy."

"Cool, let me get you your work first."

Murder walked off to the back as A-Dog looked at her.

"You got something you want to say to me A-Dog?"

"To be one hundred, you could have ran all this shit. Why didn't you step up when we knocked off Don Killer?"

"I work the back scene, A-Dog and I let a man be a man. I know people and I introduce people to people. Bitches you see run an empire is only in movies. In real life, it don't happen."

"So, what you get out of it?" asked A-Dog.

"I make friends who trust me and when I call, they answer day and night," replied Monay.

A-Dog ain't say nothing as Murder walked back in the room with two kilos for Monay.

"Here you go, Monay. Two of them, just like you asked for."

"Thank you and here ya go." Monay handed him the bag with the money inside it.

"A-Dog, here is seventy-four thousand dollars . I got to take a ride with Monay. I'll be back in a minute homie."

"Say less. You know where I'm at if you need me."

Monay looked at A-Dog. "Nice talking to you, A-Dog. I'll see you soon."

A-Dog nodded at her as they walked out.

"Where we going, Monay?" asked Murder.

"To the barbershop to see Scooby. I already told him about you."

"So, this a new trap for me?"

"Let's just say the beginning to something that can be big."

Murder ain't say nothing the rest of the ride to the barbershop. When they pulled up, Murder got out and looked around as he followed Monay inside.

"Scooby, shall we talk in the back?"

"Yeah, here I come now." Scooby walked into the back room and saw Murder sitting on the edge of the table. "What's up, Monay?"

"Scooby, let me introduce you to Murder. He's the one who supplied you with the kilos for thirty-seven thousand apiece and everybody else around here."

Scooby walked up to Murder and dapped him up.

"Peace, fam. I appreciate that business. So, I can count on you every month for two?"

"It's all love, fam. Monay told me about you already. Yeah, and you can count on me to deliver every month as long as you shopping with me and only me, agreed?" asked Murder.

"You got my word."

"Then, we in business. Take my number. Monay, you got that for him?"

"Yeah, it's in the bag right here, Murder."

Scooby took the bag from her and looked inside it and nodded.

"We good?" asked Murder.

"Yeah, we good."

Murder got up and dapped Scooby up one more time before he walked out the room. Monay looked at Murder differently as she started stepping into a boss role.

"Monay, take me to Miller Ave," Murder said.

"What's over there?"

"Your thirty percent that I have to get you from your deal."

"Okay," Monay said as she drove off.

SAYNOMORE

Chapter 33

A-Dog heard a knock at the door. He picked up his gun and went and looked out the window to see AT standing at the door. He put his gun up and opened the door.

"AT, AT, come in. What's up? How you been?"

"Good, out here trying to get a hustle on. I got twenty dollars for you now."

"You know ten or twenty, I got you. You want to make an ounce?" asked A-Dog.

"Twenty-eight grams?" AT eyes opened. When A-Dog said that she started jumping around. "How?"

"I'm looking for a nigga named Cal. He had a trap house off of Overland."

"I know exactly who you are talking about."

"I need to find him. You find out where he is for me, and I'll bless you with that ounce, ma."

"You ain't got to tell me twice. I'll know something this week."

"Good looking and you can keep this twenty. Tonight, it's on me."

AT balled her hand up, smiled and walked out the front door. She couldn't wait to get high.

***

Monay pulled up to the off-white house on Miller Ave.

"So, who house is this?" asked Monay.

"Mine, come inside. It's a safe house."

Monay stepped out the G-Wagon and followed Murder inside. She was surprised when she walked in the house at how laced it was. White and red furniture, 72-inch flat screen on the wall, white carpet.

"Murder, do you stay here?"

"No, but I keep my lights on at night to make it look good. I got drinks in the refrigerator if you are thirsty. I'll be right back with your money, Monay."

"Okay."

"Murder walked upstairs to the master bedroom. He closed the door and walked in the closet to the safe. He opened it and pulled out ten thousand dollars. He closed the safe back and walked downstairs to Monay as she looked around his house.

"Murder, this shit is fly. I like it," said Monay.

"Thanks, and here go your ten thousand dollars ."

Monay took the money and put it in her bag.

"Do you want me to bring you to the other house now?"

"Yeah, I still have a lot to do tonight."

"Murder, control the game, don't let it run you. Don Killer looked like the man, acted like the man and played the part as the man. He controlled these streets for years and never owed shit. He died a thinker. Be smarter than him. If you let the game control you, you are going to end up like him."

"You got my back, right?"

"As long as you got mines."

***

Pillz, this that fish scale for real, for real. I came by because I need another two ounces, fam. This shit going as fast as I get it."

"I told you I had that butter. Hold up, let me go get that for you, L."

Pillz walked into the backroom and pulled out the coke he had put up. He ain't notice how low he was getting. He only had a little over a quarter brick left. He picked up two ounces and walked back out there where L was waiting for him at. "Here you go playboy." Pillz handed him the ounces. L smiled when he looked at them.

"Twenty-four-hundred, right?" asked Pillz.

"Facts."

"Pillz counted the money and dapped L up. Before he left, he put the money in his pocket and pulled out his phone and called A-Dog. A-Dog picked up the phone after a few rings.

"Pillz, what's the word?" A- Dog asked.

"I got that bread and butter for you. I need another one. This shit going like hot cakes. I'm low as hell right now."

"That ain't nothing but a word. I'm about to pull up now. I'll be there in twenty or thirty minutes fam."

"Cool, I'll be waiting, Dog."

Pillz hung up the phone and went to count up the money for A-Dog.

***

Rah walked into the pool hall and up to Rock as he played a game of pool with one of his homies.

"Fellas, fellas, how's it going?" Rah asked.

"I'm just showing this new jack how to get broke calling me out on the pool table," Rock replied.

"Well look, I need to holla at you for a second, Rock," said Rah.

"This game is about to be over right now, Rah. 8 ball, corner pocket. Pay me my money, B. Cash out."

Rock picked up the $200 B threw on the pool table.

"Let me know if you want a rematch. I ain't doing shit for the next few hours. I got time to kill," replied Rock.

"You know I want that game back," said B.

"Rack them up then. I'll be right back. Rah, what's good? What you need to talk about?"

"Niggas is loving that work we got from Monay. If she letting us get them for thirty-seven, she might be getting them for thirty-three or thirty. We need to find out who her plug is because she really just the middleman, making a cap off of us."

"Man, I told you that shit the other night. You dropped the ball. You should have been trying to get in that bitch head. Her pockets are deep right now and getting fatter by the day," replied Rock.

"Look, I'm beating my feet on the ground to see who she know. You do the same and I'll call her this week for a re-up but let's see if we can go around her."

"Cool, I'll get on that now. Let me go back to getting this free money homie."

"When you ready to step your game up on the table, hit my jack."

"Nigga you right here now."

"I got moves to make but I'll pull back up," Rah laughed as he walked out the pool hall.

***

Pillz walked to the front door when he saw A-Dog pulling up. He watched as he stepped out the car with his bookbag over his shoulder as he walked in the yard.

"Da real Pillz berry, how you living baby?" A-Dog greeted.

"The good life you know me. All I do is win, win no matter what," replied Pillz.

"I hear you T-Pain."

A-Dog walked in the house and gave Pillz a pound and placed the bag on the kitchen counter.

"Here you go fam. Thirty-seven on the head."

Pillz handed A-Dog the money. A-Dog sat at the table and counted it as Pillz looked at the kilo.

"You good, Pillz?" asked A-Dog.

"Yeah, I'm about to break this bitch down now. Since Cal bounced on that ghost shit, his people been coming here."

"Well, when I catch that nigga, I'll make his ass a ghost for real."

"Look, I'm out. Clap my jack when you ready to see me again."

"Already."

A-Dog nodded as he walked out Pillz spot and to his car.

Chapter 34

Monay pulled up at the village diner. She stepped out of her Lexus and went inside. Rock was at the light when he saw her go inside. He pulled in the parking lot and got out of the car and went inside looking for her. He saw her sitting at a back table by the window, sitting by herself. He walked up to her. She looked at him when he walked up to her table.

"Can I have a seat with you?" Rock asked.

"Your name is Rock, Rahmelle's friend?" Monay followed.

"Yeah, that's me."

"Sure, have a seat. What can I do for you?"

Monay looked into Rock's eyes, but before he could say anything, the waiter walked up to the table.

"Are you ready to order?"

"Yes, I would like a coffee, three sugars, caramel creamer with the breakfast platter and an orange juice. Please Rock, order what you want, it's on me."

"I'll take the same thing she is having," replied Rah.

"Okay, your order will be out in fifteen minutes."

Monay looked back at Rock when the waiter walked away.

"As you was saying, Rock?"

"I been trying to put two and two together, but I can't. I just don't get you, Monay. This city could be yours. Why don't you want it?" asked Rock.

"Rock because I play a position where I introduce people to each other. Let me ask you this, who is more important. The puppet master or puppet?"

"The puppet master because without him the puppet can't move," replied Rock.

"You make a good point but without the puppet there wouldn't be a show. But you are wrong because the puppet master nor the puppet ain't as important as the strings. Without the strings, the puppet couldn't entertain the people. So, without the strings the puppet nor the puppet master couldn't put on a show. See Rock, I'm the strings. I'm the most important part to they act. I don't have to be the boss. My role is just as important, if not more," said Monay.

"I never looked at it that way."

"Because you only see the hood fame. Niggas that will ride your dick when they see you but you want me to tell you how they see you?"

"Yeah, how?"

"Rahmelle toy soulja. I'm not trying to be disrespectful but real. You might be the one who cook the coke up, carry the gun, trap out the house, his shooter. While he collect the money from you, make the calls to re-up and drop off back to you, until you call and tell him you out. Again, toy soulja or I can dress it up a little bit and say right hand man. You know how you know the difference? If your pockets look like his at the end of the day."

Rock just looked at Monay when she just dropped the reality ball on the table at him.

"I'm sorry for ya wait. Here are your orders," said the waiter.

"It's okay, thank you," said Monay.

"You're welcome."

"You just said some real shit, Monay, I can't even shake that shit off."

Monay took a sip of her coffee as she looked at Rock's expression on his face. She knew she had him and he was about to be a pawn on her chess board. She put her cup down.

"Now, if you think you ready for a bigger role, I could put you in that position. For a fee of course."

"What you mean?"

Monay knew she has him at that point.

"Eat Rock, this ain't the place to talk about that conversation. We will make a rain check for a later date but for now, eat your food before it gets cold," Monay said nothing else as she started to eat her breakfast.

***

AT was rushing through the path, not stopping at no one who called her name. She needed to see A-Dog or Murder. When she reached the house, she knocked two times until Murder opened the door.

"AT you are out of breath. Are you okay?" Murder quizzed with concern.

"Yeah, I was coming to let you know that I found that snake nigga Cal that you and A-Dog been looking for."

"Come in, come in. Where that nigga at?" asked Murder.

"On 45th Street, on the corner in a white house, and yes he selling drugs out of there. I was just in the car with Robin, and she just picked up from him over there."

"If what you are saying is right, we got you. I'm about to go check that shit out now."

"Okay. I told Dog that I'll find his ass," replied AT

"Say less. I got you. Let me go over there now."

"Okay."

Murder went and got his gun from the back. He locked the doors to the house, ran to his car and took off. Murder pulled up a few houses down from where AT said she saw him at. Murder pulled out his phone and called A-Dog.

"Yo Dog, where you at?"

"I'm just pulling back up to the spot. What's up?"

"I'm over here on 45th Street, AT pulled up and told me that Cal bitch ass is over here, and I just saw the fool," said Murder.

"I'm on my way over there now. Wait for me to get there before you make the move."

"Hurry up, I don't want this nigga to move."

"I'm on my way," replied A-Dog.

Murder watched as A-Dog pulled up next to his car.

"What's the word, Murder?"

"He's in the white house on the corner. I don't know who is in there with him."

"So, what's up? You want to pull up?" asked A-Dog.

"Yeah, let's do this."

Murder took off down the road with A-Dog right behind him. They both pulled up in the front yard. A-Dog jumped out of his car and ran and kicked the front door open. Murder ran in the house right behind him. Cal went to jump off the couch and A-Dog smacked him in the face with the gun. Murder saw his Pitbull run out of the back room and shot him in the head, killing him. Cal looked up from the floor with blood all over his face.

"Look at your pussy ass laying on the floor about to die for stealing my shit," Murder yelled at him. "A-Dog, check to see who else is in the house."

Murder looked around in the house from the living room, "Where the fuck is my shit at?"

In shaky voice, Cal looked up at Murder. "It's in the backroom."

A-Dog walked back to the front. "It's just him in here. I checked everywhere under the bed and all."

"Get up pussy and go get my fucking work now."

A-Dog and Murder followed him to the backroom. He moved his mattress and pulled out what was left of the brick he had.

"Where the fuck is the money at?"

"It's in the drawer right there. Come on man, please don't kill me. You got everything back," said Cal.

Murder looked at A-Dog to confirm the money was in the drawer. A-Dog put the gun to the back of Cal's head and pulled the trigger, blowing his brains on the wall. He was a ghost. Murder just looked at his dead body.

"Come on dog, let's get the fuck up out of here." Murder handed A-Dog the coke in the bag, and they walked out the house to their cars. They both got in them and drove off.

Chapter 35

Rah pulled up at the house in his old school Chevy. When he walked inside, Rock was smoking a blunt and counting money up.

"What you got right there?" asked Rah. "How much is that?"

"Twelve thousand on the head and with what I got in the back, it all comes up to twenty-seven-thousand. We got to do a count and see what they holding at J's," replied Rock.

"I'll make the call to re-up for Friday. Do the count on all the money and let me know so I'll know how much to order."

"I got you, boss, I'll take care of it."

Rah looked at Rock as he got up and walked to the back. He ain't say nothing to him he just turned around and walked out. Rock knew what Monay had said was right and Rah just proved it to him that he was the toy soulja and he was the boss.

***

Rah sat in his car and pulled out his phone to call Monay. She picked up after a few rings.

"Hey Rahmelle, it's been a while. What's up, stranger?"

"You sure I'm the stranger and not you, sexy?" replied Rahmelle.

"What's up Rahmelle. You are too much."

"I was trying to see if I could see you this week on a business tip again."

"Same thing

"No, maybe three this time."

"Okay. Let me know before Friday and we can meet up Saturday night."

"Okay. Be expecting my call sometime later today or tomorrow afternoon."

"I'll be waiting on your call, Mr. Rahmelle."

"I got you, beautiful." Rah smiled as he hung up the phone. He turned the radio up and drove off.

***

"Murder, it's good to see you again."

"It's good to see you too. Here, I have something for you."

Murder handed Omar the duffle bag. Omar looked inside and nodded as he handed the duffle bag to Pete.

"It's good. That I know. I can count on you. I can count on your word," said Omar.

"That's all we have as men and I stand on my word," replied Murder.

"I see that and respect that. So, how is business going for you so far?"

"It was a little rocky at first. A few people had to disappear to get the point across to everyone else."

Pete walked back into the office.

"Omar, it's five thousand dollars on the head." Pete spoke,

"Put everything in the car for him, please. Murder, let me know if you can take on more product because I have a never ending supply and I can provide you with whatever you want," said Omar.

"Let me work with that I have now and if the opportunity comes my way where I need a bigger shipment, I will let you know."

"Let me walk you to your car, Murder." Omar walked Murder to his car. They shook hands before Murder got in the car and drove off.

"I see you took a liking to him, boss," Pete spoke.

"He's hungry, Pete. Within the next two years, I'll be selling him a hundred kilos, trust me." Omar patted Pete on the back as he walked back into his office.

***

Monay pulled up at Radio Shack and walked in the camera department.

"Hello, Ms., May I help you?"

Monay smiled as she looked at the store clerk. "Yes, I'm looking for a small recording device."

"How small?"

"Something I could put on the arm of a chair or under a desk. Something that the eye won't notice."

"You need a bug. Come to this department. I know what you need."

Monay followed him to the other side of the store.

"Check this out. Now, this is called a bubble. You place this little ear bug anywhere in the room and whatever is said in the room automatically records on this device."

"Yes, this is exactly what I need. Thank you."

"You're welcome."

Monay walked out the store with the bag in her hand. She had one more move to make before the pieces in her plan started to come together and Rock was going to play a major part in it.

SAYNOMORE

Chapter 36

"Everything is everything, Rock?" asked Rah.

"Yeah, I broke it down in three stacks of thirty-seven thousand. If you ask me, we need to be picking up more weight. We can get ten of them a pop and just take one risk with it."

"You right, but I don't want to let her know how much we holding."

"Yeah, you right. You ready to go meet her?" asked Rock.

"Yeah, come on. She at a different spot off Greatneck Rd."

Rock put the money in the backseat of the car as he was waiting on Rah to come out the house. He turned the music up as he saw Rah coming out.

"Where we headed, Rah?"

"Take Greatneck to 110 and pull up behind Funzone. She should be there already."

"Cool."

***

"Monay, you want me to knock this nigga head off, so why you still doing business with him?" Murder spoke.

"Because it's going to benefit you in the long run. Let him build his clientele up and when you kill him and his boy Rock, the new takeover starts."

"Why you doing all this?" asked Murder.

Monay looked at Murder when he asked her that.

"Because I'm making you a made man. Plus, it's what Omar wants. Everybody at our table eats off the same plate. Omar's the plug, I'm the negotiator and you're the hustle. Nobody can lose this way. It's a win, win. We just got to knock a few players out the way. Get ready. I see the headlights of his car coming now."

Murder pulled out his gun and cocked it back as him and Monay stepped out the car with the coke in his hand.

Monay walked up to him. "Is that for me?"

"Yeah, it is. Do you have something for me?" asked Rah.

"You know I do. I'll be right back."

Monay took the backpack from Rah and walked back to her car. She took the bag from Murder and walked back to Rah.

"You're not going to count it this time?" asked Rah.

"Do I need to? I'm not worried about it. I know how to find you, Rahmelle."

"I'm sure you do."

"Take care," replied Monay as she turned around and walked off.

Rah looked at Murder from a distance as he watched Monay walk back to the car.

"Everything smooth?" asked Rock.

"Yeah, we good. Let's ride out."

***

Monay pulled up in front of Murder's trap and turned the car off.

"All the money is in the bag. He might not call for another two months, but you will have killed him and his sidekick by then."

"How long before you need that done?" asked Murder.

"I'm lining everything up."

"Say less."

Murder stepped out the car with the bag of money. He watched as Monay drove off before he walked into the house.

"Yo A-Dog, pull up."

A-Dog walked out of the backroom on the phone.

"Let me call you back, baby girl. I need to take care of something." A-Dog hung up the phone and walked up to Murder. "You ain't got no blood on you, so I'm guessing shit went smooth again?"

"Already, it's a hundred-eleven-thousand dollars in the bag. I just sold three of them to that Rahmelle nigga. You straighten AT out?"

"Yeah, she pulled up. I let her know what it was and told her the game blessed her for keeping it a hundred. I gave her the twenty-eight as promised."

"Pillz hit you up yet?"

"Hell naw. I'll give him to the end of the week," replied A-Dog.

"So, how we looking here?"

"I knocked off a few ounces. That's all but we good. We just got this new pack not even a few days ago and we already over a hundred-twenty-thousand dollars. We looking good right now."

"Big facts. You know how I am though," replied Murder, smiling.

"I be knowing, fam."

"I'm about to go put this bread up. Let me get what you made so it will be one trip."

"Hold up, let me go get that." A-Dog came back with the rest of the money and handed it to Murder.

"Thirty-six-hundred dollars."

"Facts. I'll be back, homie."

"I'll be right here."

SAYNOMORE

Chapter 37

"The beautiful Monay. What brings you by?" Omar spoke

"I just need a tune up on my car. That's all. You got me?" Monay said.

"Of course, we do. Pete will make sure it gets done. Come in my office and talk to me."

Omar placed his hand on Monay's lower back as he led her to his office.

"Please have a seat and tell me how you been?" said Omar.

"I been good, still trying to put my life back together, but I'm enjoying me now. How you been is the question?"

"Taking it one day at a time. Do you remember Murder? He was here a few times ago when you came by?"

"Yeah, I remember him. Why you ask?" replied Monay, curious.

"I just wanted to know more about him. If you can put your ears to the streets for me. He's loyal and hungry but you can never know too much about a person."

"I'll see what I can find out for you. I will have a few friends in the streets."

"Monay, I know how mad you was about Don Killer when I had you entertain him for them years to keep a close eye on him for me."

"Omar, do you know he beat me, raped me, burned my house down, treated me like shit some days? Not one time did you check him about it."

"Monay, he's dead now. Let it be the past, but I want to say thank you. I know the sacrifice you made for me."

"It is the past and we do have a much brighter future to look toward, Omar."

"That's why I love you Monay. Now, find out what you can for me on this Murder guy."

"I will."

There was a knock at the door and Pete walked in the office.

"Monay, your car is good to go." Pete said.

"Thanks, Pete and thank you, Omar."

Monay got up and walked out the office.

"Pete, we have a lot to do this week. Make sure the trucks are ready for pickup," said Omar.

"I already did. We just waiting on they end so I'll know when to go make the pickup."

"I'll make the call later today and see what the date and time will be."

"Yes sir."

***

"Yo Rock, who playing in that game tonight?" KP asked.

"Atl vs. The Bears. They playing in Atlanta." Rock answered.

KP walked into the living room where Rock was with two beers in his hand. He sat down on the couch and handed Rock a beer.

"This game going to be live. Whoever wins this game is going to make it to the playoffs. This a win or go home game, Rock."

"I be knowing already. Atl piped all the way up right now. Black and red jerseys, it's going down."

The front door opened and Rah walked in with the pizza.

"Did the game start yet?" asked Rah.

"Hell naw, it's about to kick off now. KP like the Bears. Who you like for the money?" asked Rock.

"I got to fuck with Atl. Atlanta rise up."

"That's what I'm talking about, Rah. We picking winning teams. I don't know what KP got going on."

Rock's phone went off. He looked at the text message it was from Monay.

Come meet me at Peterson Park. I'll be there in 20 minutes.

Rock replied back. *I'm on my way now to you.*

Rock jumped up. "Look, I have to make a move. I'll be back in a minute."

"You good, Rock?"

"Yeah, I'm 100, Rah. It's just some shit I need to take care of real quick."

Rock walked out the door and jumped into his car. When he pulled up to Peterson Park, Monay was standing outside of her G-Wagon. It was 7:45pm. He got out of his car and walked up to her.

"I was wondering when you was going to call me," said Rock.

"I had you in mind. I just had to make sure my end was covered. No losses," replied Monay.

"I respect that. I like how you move."

"I hope I can say the same thing about you, Rock. So, here's the deal that I'll put on the table for you. Five kilos of cocaine, ninety-seven percent pure and you re-up with me and me only. When you come to re-up, I'll let you get each one for 32 a pop. I'm giving you the work to start off with and the opportunity to become your own boss and get from underneath Rahmelle's wing."

"And what do I have to do for all of this?"

"Give the angel of death two bodies. Let's call it a death promise. You do this for me, and I'll make you a made man."

"Who is it that I got to kill?"

"Does it matter?" said Monay.

"No."

"Good. You need a silencer for your gun. You only have one shot and one shot only."

"I don't have a silencer. I have a .45 and a Glock nine-millimeter."

"Nigga, then you need to get yourself a thirtyeight and an Idaho potato and be ready for my call."

"Am I meeting you at the spot or am I riding with you?" asked Rock.

"You riding with me. I'll drop you off at the building to the shop. You going to stay ducked down when the truck pulls up, I'll call you. It's only going to be one person in the truck, kill him. When the garage doors open, another man is going to come walking out. Be on the side of the building so he don't see you. Kill him as well. Get in the truck and bring it to me right here. I'll be watching everything. You're not going to have time to pull the man out the truck after you kill him so kill him and get to the side of the building before the garage door open. Everything got to be timed just right. Do you understand?".

"Yeah."

"Good. Now, go get you a thirty-eight and potato and be ready for my call." Monay turned around, got in her G-Wagon and left without saying another word.

***

"Rock going to miss this game. Fuck a playoff, this should be a Super Bowl game. Atl defense is standing up. I don't know what you had going on with the Bears," said Rah.

"It's only twenty-one to fourteen and it's not even second half yet. It's plenty of time left. What the fuck going on? He had to make a play, you think?" asked KP.

"I don't even know. He said some shit the other day I had to brush off, but I caught it."

"What that nigga say?"

"He was calling me boss, like yeah, okay boss."

"You know what's crazy? I saw him the other morning in The Village diner and Don Killer bitch, Monay was in there."

"Shit, they was together?" asked Rah,

"She pulled in like five minutes before him, but they left out around the same time."

"You know what? Keep an eye on that nigga until we find out what's what. Something don't seem right."

"Copy that."

Rah pulled out his phone and texted Rock.

"Where you at, fam? You missing a good ass game?"

Rock replied. *"I'm on my way back now bro. Be there in 10 minutes."*

Rah put his phone in his pocket and finished watching the game.

Chapter 38

"Hello, Monay. What's up, beautiful?" Rah spoke.

"Hey, Rahmelle, what's up?" Monay replied.

"Nothing, I'm over here at J's bar having a drink. I wanted to know do you want to have a drink or play a game of pool with me?" asked Rah.

"I'm riding passed J's right now. Sure, I'll come play a game of pool with you and have a drink. I'll be there in five minutes."

"Cool, I'll see you when you get here."

Rah hung up the phone, walked to the pool table and started racking up the balls as he waited for Monay to walk in. Monay pulled up in her black Lexus at J's. She stepped out looking like a real devil as she walked into J's bar. She walked up to Rah at the pool table and gave him a hug and kiss on the cheek.

"What you drinking, beautiful?"

"Let me get a Long Island Iced Tea, Rah."

"Cool, I'll let you shoot first while I get our drinks."

"No, I'll wait for you to get back," replied Monay.

Rah nodded and walked off. Monay looked around the bar as she waited for Rah to come back.

"Here go that drink you asked for."

"Thank you. So, you ready to play Rahmelle?"

"I'm waiting on you."

Monay smiled as she took her shot. Four color balls went inside. She looked up and smiled at Rah.

"I guess I'm color, baby boy."

"I see you, Monay."

Monay and Rah played two more games before calling it quits.

"Monay, what's your story? What chapter in your book do you not want nobody to read? How did you become the person you are today?"

"What you mean, Rahmelle?"

"Real talk, your vibe and conversation is different. You are a gangsta but nobody would ever know. How did you become this person?"

Monay took a sip of her drink.

"I had to grow up fast, Rahmelle. From the age of thirteen, it was hell. My father was killed in a drug deal right before I turned thirteen. My mother was weak. She overdosed not long after my father was killed. We wasn't close to immediate family and the one person who was close, my sister, was killed the beginning of the year. But anyway, like I was saying my father's supplier took me in, but he was cold from the very beginning. He treated me no different from nobody else. School was a must, but I was fly in school every day of the week. He showed me how to hide my face behind my hand. He told me everyone will make a sacrifice. Some big, some small. When I turned nineteen, it was time for me to make my sacrifice. He introduced me to Don Killer. Don Killer broke my virginity. He treated me like a queen for the first few years."

"So, your sacrifice was to be with Don Killer, to love him?" asked Rah.

"No and yes. The real reason he wanted me to be with him was because he was supplying Don Killer with thirty kilos every three months. My job was to watch the product and his money, but Don Killer was stupid. He was taxing forty-two a kilo and he would sell wholesale. That's why he never made it to the level he could have been but after a while the fame got to him. He started treating me like shit, cheating on me, but I was blinded by love. I no longer cared about why I was really there. I was in love, and it was my downfall."

"So, you took over where he left off making your mark now?" asked Rah.

"No, I'm just introducing one person around like I was asked to do with the next few weeks I'm done."

"That's the guy you are always bringing with you to our meetings?"

"Yes."

Monay felt a vibration in her pocket. "Rah, can you excuse me I have to use the ladies room? I'll be right back."

"Sure."

164

Monay walked into the bathroom. She pulled out the device. It was blinking, letting her know there was a message on it. She listened to the message then walked back to the table where Rah was at.

"So, what about you, Rahmelle? How did you get into the game?"

"Looking up to the big homies on the block. I just wanted the fast money and live the good life when I was younger. I just ain't know that all this came with it but here I am today talking with you."

"Well, I enjoyed beating you at pool today. I really had fun, but I have to make some runs so I'll text you later."

"Yeah, do that and I enjoyed the time we spent together today."

"Likewise."

Monay walked out to her car and texted Rock.

"Be ready Thursday at 4pm. I'll pick you up at 2pm be ready."

Rock replied back.

"I'll be ready when you come get me."

Monay put her phone down and drove out the parking lot to Murder's trap. She needed to talk with him.

***

"A-Dog I'm about to go see Mac. I'll be back in a few hours."

"No, we need somebody here. We don't need to miss no money if we trying to make this goal. every penny counts."

"Say less. Hit my line if you need me."

"You already know I'll hit you when I'm on my way back."

"Copy that."

A-Dog sat down on the couch and rolled a blunt up when he heard a knock at the door. He got up and looked through the peephole and saw Monay standing there. He unlocked and opened the door.

"Monay, what's up? Come in."

"Hey A-Dog, is Murder here?"

"No, he had to take a trip out of town."

A-Dog closed the door as he looked at Monay's body.

"Is there something I can do for you?"

"You remember the deal we had if I helped you get Don Killer?" asked Monay.

"Yeah, I do."

"Well, I'm calling on my end to be covered now on Thursday."

"I'll take care of it for you. Murder already got too much on his plate. Just tell me where I need to be at?"

Monay looked at A-Dog. "You sure?"

"Big facts. What he can't wash with his hands, I will with mine."

"I'll come get you at 1pm and put you where you need to be. When he step out the truck, I just need you to pull the trigger and dump the body."

"Cool, I'll be waiting on your call," said A-Dog.

"No, don't wait on my call. Just be ready at 1pm when I pull up to catch a body."

"I'll be here waiting on you then."

Monay smiled as she walked out the door to her car.

***

Rock sat on the hood of his car, drinking a 40 ounce of beer and smoking a Newport when Rah walked up to him.

"You smooth, fam?" asked Rah.

"Hell yeah. I'm thinking about our next move."

"Word, what you come up with?"

"We need Albany Ave, Smith Street and everything over there. It's time for us to get our hands dirty. Rah, we should be about to move two bricks within a month."

"You right, but we don't need all that heat on us right now. They just found a body in a house on 45th Street. Within the last year, The Ville been hot ever since 2.5 and Ammo got setup and killed and all the bullshit that came behind it. It just ain't the right time," explained Rah.

"If we keep waiting, it's never going to be the right time. Then, them niggas gon' ride down on us too. I'll be looking at your body in a casket or you looking at mine," replied Rock.

"Look, don't even think like that. Niggas know who we are in these streets, and they know our guns go off."

"That's the thing, Rah. The streets are starting to forget, just look around. It's 1pm. I got a play I need to make. I'll pull up on you later, fam."

"Meet me at J's when you done, fam."

"Sure, I'll be there."

Rah watched as Rock got in his car and drove off.

***

Monay was at Peterson Park when Rock pulled up. He stepped out his car and got into the black Ford Explorer she was in.

"You ready, Rock?" asked Monay.

"Yeah, I am." Rock showed her the .38 with the potato on it.

"I see you are ready. It's one man in the white truck. Do I have to go over the details again?"

"No, I got them. I'll do my part. Just put me where I need to be," replied Rock.

"I like the attitude. Let's ride. Now, remember, get to the side of the building. I'll call you when I see the truck coming your way."

"Say less."

Rock put the murder one mask over his face as Monay dropped him off by the woods. She drove off to wait until the other parking lot to wait on the truck to come down the road. She looked at the time, it was 3:45PM. She'd only been sitting for five minutes before she saw the truck coming down the road. She called Rock." It's coming to you now. Be ready."

"I already am."

Rock hung up the phone and pulled his gun out. Pete pulled up to the back of the shop in the white Escalade. He stopped at the back doors and blew the horn twice. Rock ran up to the side of the truck door and opened it up. Pete looked at him right before he blew his brains out, making his body go limp. He closed the door to the truck and ran to the side of the building as he watched the garage doors open. Omar stepped out. Rock ran up to him and shot him in the chest, dropping him. Omar looked up at him.

"Do you know who the fuck I am?" Omar asked.

"Yeah, a dead man." Rock followed.

Rock shot him two more times in the head, killing him. He ran to the truck and pulled Pete's body out. He jumped in the truck and pulled off, following Monay to the warehouse. Once they drove both trucks inside the warehouse, Monay stepped out of the Explorer and walked to the Escalade. As Rock stepped out, he took his murder one mask off. A-Dog came from the side.

"Yo, son."

When Rock turned around, A-Dog was already letting shots off in his chest. Rock's body fell to the ground. A-Dog stood over top of him and shot him five more times in the chest, killing him.

"Now what?" asked A-Dog.

"You get rid of the body," replied Monay.

"Where you want me to dump it at?"

"I don't give a fuck. Avon Lake, the back of a store dumpster, it's up to you. Just make sure he has the gun on him when you dump him."

A-Dog went to get the stolen car he had and put Rock's body inside of it. He nodded at Monay.

"You good?"

"Yeah, I'm good. I'll catch up to you later."

A-Dog got in the car and drove off. Monay walked to the garage door and closed it. She got in the Escalade and put the radio on 106.5. She turned the AC on and then the fog lights. That's when you heard the double floor pop out. She stepped out and opened the back door to the truck and moved the thick floor and was looking at 300 kilos of cocaine.

Chapter 39

Murder was watching the news. He couldn't believe what he was hearing. They were running the story on Omar shop. They were talking about how Omar Knox and Pete Christen Miller were killed at the shop Thursday afternoon shot down when A-Dog walked in the house.

"Damn, why you look like that bro?" A-Dog asked.

"Omar and Pete was gunned down yesterday afternoon. That was the plug." Murder spoke.

"Fuck no, you sure?"

"Look it's right here on the news. They talking about it now."

"Damn, how much we holding now?"

"No more than twelve bricks right now."

"Who the fuck you think did this?"

"I don't know. Let me call Monay."

Murder called Monay. She picked up on the first ring.

"Murder, let me call you back. I'm watching the news. This is not going to end well."

"I'm watching the news now, too."

"Yeah, I have to make some calls to find out something. Murder, once I do, I'll call you back."

"Okay, I'll be waiting on your call."

Murder hung up the phone and continued to watch the newscast on Omar's murder.

***

"Yo, Rah?" KP called.

"What's up, KP?" Rah answered.

Rah looked at KP's facial expression. He knew something was wrong.

"Rock was killed last night. They just found his body behind Home Depot, He was gunned down."

"What the fuck you mean gunned down. By who?" asked Rah.

"I don't know, bro. They flatlined son."

"Come on, somebody have to tell me something. I was just with him yesterday. Niggas want some, let's give it to them."

Rah ain't say nothing as he drove his car, thinking about the last conversation him and Rock had with each other. Now, he was going to be looking at his man in a casket.

"Yo KP, do you know who he was with last week?"

"The last time I seen him was the night of the game."

"Who called and told you about him being killed?" asked Rah.

"Alex said he saw it on the news with two other murders this morning."

***

Monay called Murder back and before the phone made it to the second ring, he picked up.

"Yeah, I do. It was a conflict between him and his partner. You smart, you know how the rest of the story go."

"Yeah, what are we going to do now?" asked Murder.

"I'm trying to work something out for you now. Just give me a while to put some things together."

"Cool, just let me know something."

"I will as soon as I know something."

Murder hung up the phone and rolled a blunt up.

"Yo' A-Dog, what was you telling me about yesterday?"

Monay came here looking for you two days ago, but you wasn't here. It was about that nigga, Rah. Long story short, she set it up yesterday where I knocked off the nigga Rock, Rah's man."

"Word, where at?" asked Murder.

"Some warehouse. I flatlined him and dropped his body off behind Home Depot."

"What about the nigga, Rah?"

"She ain't say nothing about him, fam."

"Cool, I'm about to smoke this blunt and get my thoughts together. We need a plug bad."

"Say less."

***

Rah sat on the corner of the pool table, taking shots of Cîroc as he talked to KP.

"Rah, we got to look at two pictures here. Rock was moving reckless. You even said it yourself. You caught him saying slick shit. He was saying he got to make plays, not putting us on or letting us know what he was doing, real shit. He started being for himself."

"So, what you saying? He deserved what happened to him?" asked Rah.

"Hell no, I'm not, but he should have been right here with us. He ain't even let you know where he was going before he left. Like I said, he was moving reckless."

"And he was talking reckless, saying he wanted to take over Smith Street and Albany Ave. The last thing he told me was if we don't make a move soon, one of us is going to be in a casket and the other one is going to be looking down at the body in the casket. Now my nigga dead, fuck."

"Look, we going to find out who did this shit, but right now, we need to stay on point with a clear mind. We could end up stiff on a cold plate of steel," replied KP.

Yeah, you right. The streets will be talking in a few days. I'm about to ride out, KP. I'll hit your line tomorrow."

"Be safe out there, Rah."

"Already."

***

"Detective Josephs, let me have a word with you for a second."

Detective Josephs went into Scott's office and closed the door behind him.

"What you got for me, Mr. Scott?" asked Detective Josephs.

"Kevin Walker aka Rock."

"Yeah, what about him?"

"He had a gun on him with gun residue all over his hands, and clothes. I ran a ballistic test on the gun and it's the same one who killed Omar Knox and Pete Christen Miller.

"He's your killer that you are looking for," said Scott.

"Who else did you tell this to?"

"Nobody."

"Good, keep it that way. We never had this conversation, Detective."

"What conversation?"

Detective Joseph walked into his office and pulled up all know affiliations tied to Kevin Walker name. He quickly saw Terror Squad head member Rahmelle Stone aka Rah. Detective Joseph printed out everything on Rahmelle Stone and walked out of his office to his car. He pulled out his phone and made a call.

"Hey, it's me. I found our guy but he's dead. I do have the information to the one who might have called the shot. He's a known drug dealer around here. Okay, okay. I'm sending you all the information now."

Detective Joseph took pictures of everything he printed out and sent it to who he was talking to before driving off.

Chapter 40

"Pillz, how the motivation coming over here?"

"Like clockwork, A-Dog,"

"You ready for me again?" asked A-Dog.

"You know that's why I called you. They loving this butter. I got seventy-four-thousand dollars. Let me get two of them off you," replied Pillz.

"I only brought one with me now. Let me grab that off you and I'll be back later with the other one."

"Let me go get the bag. I'll be right back."

A-Dog looked around the trap as he waited for Pillz to come back.

"Yo, yo, it's right here, fam. Seventy-four grand in the bag."

"Cool. I'll be back in maybe two or three hours with the other brick."

"Say less, A-Dog."

"A-Dog gave Pillz a pound before walking out the spot. Once in the car, he called Murder.

"I just left Pillz. He had seventy-four for us. I only brought one to him. He needs one more."

"Cool, I'm at the spot now. I'll bring it to him. You on your way back now?" asked Murder.

"Yeah."

"Well, you know where everything is at. I'm about to head over to him now with that other one."

"Copy that."

A-Dog drove off bumping Jay-Z's *Black Album*.

***

Monay sat at her table in her bedroom and removed 3 pieces of her chess board and moved 2 pieces before getting up. Karma was a bitch, and she knew that. Every piece on her chess board owed Karma a debt and she was collecting for the bitch. They all cost her pain. She looked in the mirror at her reflection and saw two faces and knew one of them was innocent and she accepted that. She respected the person she became. No, she respected the person they made her.

***

Detective Josephs walked outside the police station to smoke a cigarette when his phone went off.

"Hello."

"Can you talk, Detective?"

"Yeah, I can."

"Take care of this problem."

"What about the package?" asked Detective Josephs.

"It's plenty more where that came from. It won't be the first loss we took in this business, but don't nobody walk away knowing they took from us."

"Okay, I'll get on it ASAP."

"Detective, make it sooner than later because we don't want nothing like this to happen again. We don't need them to think they got away with this, you got me?"

"Yes sir."

"Good. Call me when it's done."

"Will do."

Detective Josephs hung up the phone and walked to his car and drove off.

***

Murder called Monay as he sat on the hood of his car, smoking a blunt.

"Hey, Murder."

"What's good, Monay. You busy?"

"No, I was on my way to get something to eat. Do you want to meet me at The Village diner?" asked Monay.

"Sure, I'll be there in ten minutes."

Murder hung up the phone, got in his car and drove off to meet Monay. He pulled up a few seconds before she did. He watched as the white G-Wagon pulled into the parking lot. He opened his car door as she got out her truck. Monay walked up and gave Murder a light hug.

"Come, let's go order our food. I'm so hungry right now."

"So, you come here all the time?" asked Murder.

"Since I was a little girl. This is my favorite spot to eat."

"I wanted to ask you did you ever find a new source for us?"

"Hold on one second, Murder. Kim, can you bring us two of my regulars please?" asked Monay.

"Sure will."

"Thank you. I just ordered our food. Trust me, you are going to love it. And I have been making calls, but right now the detail shop is being watched from what I was told. So, you might want to stretch what you have for now to make it last until something comes our way."

"Yeah, I said that to myself last night. You don't think Don Killer had a stash somewhere that we can get. That house was big as hell."

"To tell you the truth, I don't know. That house went into foreclosure. He didn't even own it. His family got most of his things out that house," replied Monay.

"I thought you lived there?" asked Murder.

"Oh no never, but don't worry. Something will come through soon, trust me."

"A-Dog told me about the other night, too."

"Yes, I came looking for you. I told him what need to be done and he said he will take care of it. He is very loyal to you, Murder."

"And I'm just as loyal to him as he is to me. So, what about the other member to the party?"

"I'll reach out to him this weekend and set that up for us."

Murder ain't say nothing as Kim walked to the table with their trays.

"Here you two go."

"Thank you," said Murder.

"You're welcome."

"So, when he's gone, we got his clientele are just going to need to be able to supply them if anything."

"We will cross that bridge when it comes. Now, let's eat. My stomach is touching my back, Murder."

Murder smiled as he started to eat.

Chapter 41

"Rah, you good homie?"

"Yeah, one hundred, KP. I'm just setting this play up for tonight at Cloud Nine."

"Shit, you going to the club tonight?" asked KP.

"Yeah, I'll swing through before it open just to handle this business. Then, I'm out," replied Rah.

"Shit, it's already six. The club open up at eight. What time you rolling through?"

"In about an hour, I'm rolling out. I can't lie. I'm still fucked up over Rock, KP and not knowing who did the shit is really killing me."

"That shit going to come to the light soon. Shit like that always do."

"Yeah, I just wish I knew who he was meeting up with. That shit would put light at the end of the tunnel."

"Look, you want me to ride with you, bro?"

"No, I'm good. I'm about to pull out now. I'll see you when I get back.

"Cool, you know where to find me at."

Rah gave KP a pound before leaving to J's Bar.

***

Murder walked Monay out of the diner, "So where you headed now?"

"I don't know where I am about to go, Murder. What about you?"

"I have to go to work on stretching the rest of what I got until you hear something."

"Okay, I'll call you when I hear something and if I can set that up for the weekend, Murder."

"Okay, call my line, Monay."

"I will."

Monay got into her truck and drove off. When Rah saw her, he followed her through Village. Monay saw him and turned off into the library parking lot. Monay stepped out her truck with her gun in her hand as she walked up to Rah's car.

"Is there a fucking reason you following me?"

"Damn, you walking up with hammer in your hand. I was just trying to get your attention," replied Rah.

"Shit, you got it now, what's up?" asked Monay.

"Look, I need to see you again on the business tip."

"Look, call my phone and we will go from there."

Monay turned around and got into her truck and drove off. Rah just looked at her. He ain't respect what she just did. He promised himself he was going to check her about that shit the first chance he got. And if she got wrong, he was going to body her ass. Rah pulled up at Cloud 9. He stepped out the car and knocked two times on the side door. He stepped back as the door opened.

"Rah, come in, fam."

"Tug, what it do bro?" said Rah as he dapped Tug up.

"I have that paperwork for you in the backroom. Follow me bro."

Rah followed Tug to the backroom.

"So, look Tug, shit getting low right now. So, this is the last one for a minute, fam," said Rah.

"Do you know how long?"

"Hell naw, but you know when it comes through I got you ASAP. I'll hit your jack."

"I be knowing. Won't you stay and party with me tonight. I heard about Rock. You need to clear your mind up. Have a few drinks with me, dog," replied Tug.

"Some other time. I have some more runs to do tonight before it gets too late."

"Cool, I respect that. Here you go. Forty-two grand."

Rah counted the money and placed it in the bag before walking out the room. He put the bag in the backseat of the car before driving off. He pulled out his phone and called KP.

"Yo, I'm on my way back now from J's."

"Everything work out?" asked KP.

"Cool, I'll see you when you get here then."

"Cool."

***

Chief Locks was sitting behind his desk when one of the officers walked into his office.

"Excuse me, Chief."

"Yes come, how can I help you?"

"This just came in the mail. You might want to see this."

"Sure, what is it?"

The officer handed the CD to the Chief Locks. Chief Locks put it in the laptop on his desk.

"You got to be fucking kidding me. Get Smith down here now."

"Yes sir."

When Detective Smith walked into Chief Lock's office, Chief Locks shows him the video tape of Murder standing over Don Killer, talking about the killing of the two police officers earlier that year. And then you saw Murder kill Don Killer, shooting him in the head before walking out of the house.

"Boom Chief, we got him red handed, confessing his part in the cop killings and Don Killer."

"Get an APB out on him right now, dead or alive. I want his ass now."

"Yes, sir."

Chief Locks couldn't believe how this video just fell into his hands.

***

Rah walked into J's Bar up to the bar.

"Yo, can I get some chicken fingers, fries and a Coors lite?"

"What's up? You down for a game of pool until your food ready bro?"

"Yeah, I'm down. Come on. Damn, you always want to play and lose, but shit I like free money, baby boy."

"Yo Rah, who the fuck is that by your car dressed in all black like that?" asked KP.

"The fuck if I know. Come on."

Rah ran out the bar doors.

"Yo, yo." The man took off running a little ways, then stopped and turned around. Rah stopped when he saw the barrel of the .45 in his face. He couldn't move as the bullets ripped through his body. KP jumped behind a car as the man stood over the top of Rah and shot him five times, killing him before taking off running. When KP came from behind the car, he walked up to Rah's lifeless body, lying in a pool of blood.

"Fuck man. Fuck! Not you too, homie." KP couldn't believe what just happened that quick as he looked down at Rah shaking his head. You heard the police sirens coming from the distance to the crime scene. KP just stood there. He couldn't move, looking at his man dead.

Chapter 42

A-Dog came from the backroom, holding his phone in his hand.
"Shit crazy right now, Murder. Pillz just hit my line and said that somebody flatlined Rah last night at J's bar."
"Dead ass."
"I'm about to call him right now to see what happened."
"Do that," said Murder.
Pillz pick the phone up on the first ring.
"Pillz, what went down?" asked A-Dog.
"I don't even know, Dog. I just got word he got clapped. That shit is all over Facebook and the Gram."
"They ain't say who did it?"
"Nah, all they said was that someone tried to break into his car. He took off chasing them and they turned around and started clapping him. That's all they said," replied Pillz.
"Cool, let me tell Murder, fam."
"Copy that."
A-Dog walked up to Murder and saw he was on the phone already.
"Yeah, Monay. They said our weekend party got canceled already last night at J's Bar."
"Let me check into that and I'll call you right back Murder."
"Cool, let me know something and don't forget to hit me back on that tip."
"I won't. I'm getting on that now."
Monay hung up the phone, smiled and removed one more piece off her chest board as she took a sip of her wine. She turned on the news as she waited for the last two pieces to unfold to her plan.
***
AT walked through the path as fast as possible to A-Dog trap house. She knocked two times on the door before Murder answered.
"What's up AT?"
"Boy it is fucking hot as hell out here right now. You got them police everywhere out there right now riding around."
"Damn, what the fuck is going on out there?" asked Murder.

"I don't know child but here I got fifty dollars. Do me right. I ain't trying to come back out."

"You know I got you, AT"

Murder opened the cabinet and pulled out a sack of dope and weighed up a gram and handed it to AT

"Look it's too hot right now. I'm closing the trap down so it's over with for the day," said Murder.

"Shit, I don't blame you. If you would see how it is out there," replied AT

"Be safe out there, AT"

"You too, Murder."

AT walked back through the path to Smith Street to go to the red house.

"Yo A-Dog, check me out. I just closed the trap for the day. The block is hot. Police is everywhere. AT just told me."

"The police is here, Murder. Come look out the window. They got a stakeout on our spot."

"Oh shit, how much we got in the house?" asked Murder.

"Like a quarter brick. If that much."

"A-Dog, you know this shit is going to end bad for us. I'm letting you know that I'm going out blazing."

"Guns up then, I'm riding with you."

"Look, we are going to run to the cars. You go to the left. I'm going to the right. I love you, Dog."

"I love you more, Murder."

Murder and A-Dog hugged each other one last time.

"Go."

A-Dog ran outside and jumped off the steps with Murder right behind him. Murder jumped into his Charger and took off with A-Dog right behind him. Murder made a right on Sunrise Hwy. He had two police cars chasing him. A-Dog hit the back road without them seeing him.

"Y'all motherfuckers want me, come and get me," said Murder to himself. He hit the ramp to go to 110 with three more cop cars chasing him. He looked back and got side swiped. His car flipped over and rolled twice. He was dizzy from the impact as he climbed out the car, gun in hand.

"Freeze, freeze. Drop the gun! Don't fucking move." Murder looked around at all the guns pointed at him. "I'm not going to say it again. Drop the gun,"

Murder looked and saw the black BMW doing about 50 miles per hour coming from the other direction. As soon as they started to shoot at him, A-Dog stopped in front of him. He jumped in the car. A-Dog took off.

"You should have left me," said Murder.

"Fuck that! They kill you, they kill me. We in this shit together."

A-Dog stopped the car when he saw the roadblock in front of them.

"You ready Murder?"

"Yeah."

A-Dog floored it as fast as he could. The car took multiple gun shots. A-Dog rammed the police car head on. The impact of the car knocked him out. Murder opened the car door and started shooting at the police and was hit in the shoulder. He dropped his gun and was hit in the back. He fell to his knees. They rushed him and cuffed him. He looked from the side of his face as he was on the ground and saw A-Dog being put in the ambulance. They shackled his feet too. He just closed his eyes as they carried him away.

SAYNOMORE

Chapter 43

Two months later…

Murder sat down in the attorney's booth as he watched the video tape of him killing Don Killer and talking about his part in the police shooting that left two officers dead.

"Here's the deal Alex, you are looking at the death sentence. They have you dead to the wrong killing a man point blank range. Then, you are talking about your involvement in killing two police officers. Even though you ain't kill them, you were a part of it, so you are just as guilty. Then, the shootout with the police on 110. They got you with attempted murder on more than one police officer. There's no winning this case. The DA wants the death sentence, but she will take three life sentences plus eighty-five years. That's the plea. There is no other offer on the table."

"Mr. Wright, we can't get a hung jury."

"No, they got you on tape."

"What's going on with Anthony? How is he?"

"He's still in a coma."

"What they got him charged with?"

"Nothing that's going to get him more than five years at the most. We are talking about you right now."

"Okay, I'll take the deal."

"Smart choice. I can't say I know the feeling, but in time, you will make peace with your choice you made. I'll see you next week to take your plea."

"Okay."

Murder was back in his cell. He was laying on the bed thinking about everything as all the pieces started to make sense to him. How Monay set him up from the jump and he never saw it. He started thinking from the very beginning from when she first came to the house. She told him that Don Killer would be there. She walked out the room when they came in so she wouldn't be on camera when the killed him. She was recording it from the other room. She made it seem like Don Killer tipped off the police on Omar that's why BG was killed there.

Then, he remembered seeing her truck when he was out of town. She ain't want to see him, she wanted to see A-Dog. She convinced A-Dog to kill Rock but not Rah. A-Dog told him it was a white Escalade in the warehouse when he killed Rock. He got out of it, and she told him to make sure he had the gun on him when he dumped the body. Fuck because she had Rock kill Omar and Pete, knowing that the gun was going to come back as the murder weapon. And whatever cops worked for Omar would find out and makes it look like Rah had Omar killed. That's why he was gunned down and I remember Omar saying a new shipment was coming in soon. That's why she had Rock bring the truck back to the warehouse so she can get it. And the last thing she did was send the video tape to the police and got me and A-Dog locked up. She been planning this from the beginning. She set us all up to kill each other off. It's because of her Don Killer wanted 2.5 and Ammo killed. That's what Trap was talking about. Murder laid on the bed looking at the ceiling, thinking how Monay triple crossed everybody and walked away the winner.

***

Monay walked into the cemetery with Rah and white roses in her hands. She walked up to her best friend's tombstone and laid down the roses.

"RIP beautiful. I love you and miss you so much. I got everyone who was a part of your death back and Murder is doing life in prison. Death was too easy for him."

Monay kissed her two fingers and touched Tasha's headstone before leaving the cemetery. As she drove off, a sun shower started. When she looked in her rearview mirror, a rainbow was over the cemetery. She smiled to herself as she drove home.

Law Number 2

Never put too much trust in friends. Learn how to use enemies.

Pillz sat in the house watching the news about the car chase that came to a standoff with Amityville Police Department on 110. He watched as Murder was handcuffed and A-Dog was taken to Southside Hospital behind the bullshit that took place over the last year. He knew just like Murder and A-Dog death, or prison was already promised to them in the end. Pillz cut the TV off and rolled up a blunt. He looked at the two kilos of cocaine he had on the kitchen table, knowing he has to stretch them out and break them down. There wasn't no love for the block. Both his homies were down bad so he had to step it up now. He picked up his gun when he heard a knock at his front door.

"Who is it?"

"Faith."

Pillz walked to the front door and opened it. "What's good, Faith. Come in, baby girl."

Faith walked into the house after Pillz closed the door. He walked up to her and gave her a friendly hug.

"Pillz, I smell the gas in the air. Let a bitch smoke with you."

"The blunt is in the ashtray. Go ahead and relight it up."

"I came by because I was watching the news and I saw the homies going out blazing. That was fucked up how shit went down with Murder and A-Dog. They playing that shit all over the news."

"Yeah, I was just watching it. Shit it crazy right now and they saying they have a video of Murder killing Don Killer and admitting to the police killings a year ago. If they have all what they are saying, it's over for the kid".

Faith nodded and passed the blunt to Pillz.

"I don't know what to say on that note. I just wish the homies the best of luck, but I also need to get a little twenty-eight grams from you if you got it."

"I do but after this, I'm taxing but I got you for twelve hundred right now."

"Good looking. How much you taxing so I'll know next time?"

"Sixteen hundred for the twenty-eight grams."

"I can work with that."

"Cool. Let me go weigh that up for you right now." Pillz walked off as Faith sat at the table counting her money out. When Pillz walked back into the kitchen, Faith handed Pillz the money. She watched as he counted it up before putting it into his pocket.

"That's pure cocaine you have right there."

"Ya already know. It's that ninety percent pure you can cut it twice and them baseheads will still be banging at your door like they are the jump out boys." Faith just nodded and watched as Pillz weighed everything up.

"Yo, baby girl. Twenty-eight grams on the head."

"I see. I see. I'm glad we still got a real nigga holding the block down."

"And I'm not going nowhere and that's on Browns."

"I'm hold you to that shit too, Pillz."

"Say less Faith." Pillz hugged Faith one more time before she walked out the front door. He locked the door and walked back into the kitchen to break everything down.

***

Monay had all 300 kilos on the table in the basement of her house. She had a wall safe placed in her basement in the last room to the right that was six feet tall and could hold them to see was ready to move them. She knew it was only a matter of time before Big Country would send someone up to Omar's detail shop to find out what happened to his shipment and who killed his men. If she knew Big Country like she thought she, did it would be Manny who would take the trip to Long Island, NY to Omar's detail shop. So, she knew she would have to play it smart. She knew by having Omar killed all that was going to come behind it. She started walking the kilos to the safe from the table.

***

"Shit is crazy right now LA. Rah dead, Rock dead and we don't know who the fuck did it. We don't have no work."

"Just chill out, Shawn, Mase is out there right now trying to get shit together my guy. This is just a small setback and if we have to kick in a nigga door, so be it. It is what it is to get the team back on our feet. I'm always down for the one-eighty-seven."

"I'm just trying to eat. I don't give a fuck who has to take a dirt nap. Too many of my homies got caught down bad anyway. So, I'm for the fuck shit.

"And you already know I'm right here with you."

"So, have that fool Mase pulled up on Shawn?"

"Real talk, what we don't know won't hurt us. That's that man business. I'm just waiting to see what he brings to the table." Shawn started to roll up a blunt when his phone went off. He looked and saw it was a message from Mase telling him to meet him at the bar.

"Yo LA. We just talked that boy up. Mase hit my line and said we need to meet him at the bar."

"About fucking time. Come on, Shawn. Let's see what the fuck he's talking about. I'm ready to get to this fucking paper. My pockets are on empty right now."

"Stop tricking off on them bitches and you won't be broke, super save a ho nigga."

"You got me fucked up. The only thing I trick off on a bitch with is condoms."

"Yeah, I know that's right. I hear you my guy." LA looked at Shawn as they walked out the door to his car.

"You know what Shawn, you ain't shit."

"Yeah, I know that already but what you won't be able to call me is a trick." LA bit his bottom lip and smiled at Shawn as he got into his car.

SAYNOMORE

Chapter 44

Manny walked around to the back of the detail shop and saw where Pete was killed. The blood stain was still on the ground. Just as Omar's blood stain was still at the back door.

"Jake, someone knew about this shipment. This was a planned hit. They knew that Omar and Pete was going to be alone."

"Manny, I thought they killed the guy who called the hit on Omar?'

"Yeah, me too but I think there is more to it then we know. We are talking about three hundred kilos. Think about this, Jake. Fifty kilos wholesale is one point five million. There is someone who has three hundred kilos of Big Country's and is looking at sevnteen million dollars of his money out here."

"Is Monay still up here? She was Omar's property at one point in time."

"Yeah, like you just said, at one point in time. From the time she was a little bitch, I didn't trust her, but she was loyal to Omar. Even the most loyal dog will bite the owner's hand at some point in time. Let's just hope that's not the case here."

"Are you going to reach out to Monay?"

"For what? She know what lines to cross. Come on. Let's go check out the inside now." Jake walked in front of Manny as they entered the detail shop.

***

Pillz was walking down Albany Ave. smoking a blunt when AT walked up to him.

"Pillz, when is the candy shop going to open back up?"

"AT, the candy shop is already open. It's just on Bayview now."

"Next time, it would be nice to let a bitch know."

"I got you, baby girl."

"You got something on you now?"

"Yeah, what you looking for?"

"I have twenty dollars on me now?"

"Come over here and I got you." Pillz walked AT to the side of the building as he gave her something for $20. Monay watched him from across the street in her black BMW. She got Murder and A-Dog out the way. Now, she just had to put her strings on to Pillz and make him her puppet but for her to do that Murder has to be all the way out of the picture. Plus, it was only a matter of time before Murder put two and two together. So, death was the only promise she knew that would keep his mouth closed. Pillz turned around just in time to see the black BMW drive off.

***

Mase sat at the bar looking at the game when LA and Shawn walked into the bar.

"Yo, Mase, you don't even have to finish watching that game. We all know that the Giants are going to lose."

"Damn, I love a hating ass nigga." Mase looked dead into LA eyes when he said that. He got up and walked to the pool table with LA and Shawn right behind him.

"So, here is the move. The block is dry and the only nigga who got weight right now is Pillz. I don't know how much he is holding but I do know that the block is fucking with him."

"So, you saying we need to pull up on Pillz with the fuck shit?"

"No LA. I'm not saying that. What I'm saying is we need to find out who his plug is and if he don't want to tell us, then we get on the fuck shit with him." Shawn looked at both, not saying a word.

"Real shit, we need to go another way. Pillz ain't going to turn no stick niggas onto his plug dead ass."

"So, then fuck that nigga. If he ain't trying to tell us who his plug is, then we just lay his ass down and take his shit. Like you said, he ain't one of us."

"Look, LA. I'm go talk with him to see what he talking about. Me and Pillz go way back so I got this." Mase looked at Shawn.

"Make sure you make the point that we need to know where we can cop from, or the next conversation won't be friendly."

"Yeah, I got this, Mase."

"I know you do, Shawn."

***

"Put your money on the concrete or close your fucking mouth. Now, put your bets down niggas. $20 or better and you better hurry up before I roll these fucking dice."

"Man, fuck what you are talking about. You talking big money. Let me shut this nigga the fuck up." Pillz pulled out $2,000 and dropped it on the concrete.

"Nigga, two G's on the concrete. I don't care if you put it in twenty dollars, fifty dollars, or a hundred dollars. Let's see how much faith you have in your roll."

"Baby boy, you ain't saying shit. Four, five, six on the come out gettem girls." JT rolled the dice as he snapped his fingers watching the dice hit the wall and bounce off it.

"Four, five, six my ass, nigga. You better try one, two three. Pay me my coins, JT. I need that bread in my life like a bad bitch in high heels." Pillz laughed as he picked the money up from the ground.

"I see you over here still breaking pockets, Pillz."

"Shawn, what's rocking my guy? Long time, no see. You trying to put some bread down on the concrete?"

"No, I really just came to talk some business with you."

"Shit, walk with me over here. What's good?"

"Look Pillz, niggas ain't trying to step on your toes but I'm pulling up to see if you can link me in with your plug. We trying to eat too on the other side of Greatneck Rd. fam."

"Real talk, I'm only eating off of what Murder and A-Dog left me. I really need to find a plug too."

"So, what can you sell me weight wise?"

"I might be able to do a half of bird for twenty-one G's. That's the best I can do, fam."

"You can't do the whole thing."

"Hell to da no. That's a big ass dub."

"Cool. I'll pull up and let LA and Mase know the move and I'll be in touch.

"Yeah, you know where to find me at homie. This offer ain't going to be on the table for too long." Pillz just watched as Shawn walked off.

"Money on the pavement. What the fuck ya niggas trying to lose?" Pillz yelled.

Chapter 45

"Yo, Shawn. What your man's talking about?"

"He said he can fuck with us on the half a bird for the twenty-one. That's the best he can do." LA looked at Mase when Shawn said that.

"That nigga trying us on some cornball shit. Twenty-one for half a bird, Mase. You hear this nigga?"

"Yeah, I hear him. Shit, I'm sitting right here with you. So, what you saying is he not going to turn us onto his plug and we dead on the whole bird?"

"Man, I'm saying we just pop this nigga and take his shit. Fuck using our mouthpiece. We need to let the four pound do the talking now and whatever the fuck nigga have we walking up out of there with."

"Real shit, Shawn. I'm with LA on this one. We tried it your way, now it's our way."

"I ain't down for it. You niggas can do two deep on that move. I'm good."

"So, what you are saying is fuck how we eat as long as that nigga is good. So, you going against the home team, Shawn for the Albany Ave. nigga?"

"LA, you always trying to throw some shit into the game. You know where the fuck I stand at."

"I don't know shit."

"Keep that same energy too, nigga."

"Always big fucking facts, super save a nigga."

"You know what LA? You are a fucking clown." Shawn looked at both of them as he smiled and walked out of the house.

"Mase, that nigga is going to be our downfall."

***

"Manny, do you realize there are no cameras in here. We don't even know who Omar was doing business with." Manny pulled out a black book from Omar's desk and placed it on top of the desk and showed Jake everybody's name they was doing business with.

"This book shows he's been doing a lot of business with this Murder and A-Dog. Now, we just need to know who they are."

"I'll get on that right now. I remember the cop Omar had on his payroll. I'll reach out to him."

"Yeah, see what you can find out. We need to get things lined up and pick back up where Omar left off at."

I'ma go make some calls now."

***

"Where this nigga at?"

"On gang. I'm willing to bet this fool is in Overland, LA."

"So, shit that's where we headed. Pull up game strong. We jumping out, gripping so this nigga Pillz get the fucking picture.

Pillz was walking down Overland, smoking a blunt and texting on his phone when Blue walked up on him."

"Pillz, two things I know about you."

"Word, and what's that Blue?"

"You going to stay with a blunt in your mouth and stay getting that money."

"Blue, you making me sound like the block boy of the year."

"I'm just calling it how I see it, Pillz."

Both started to laugh. Blue looked past Pillz at the black SUV that pulled over to the side of the road as Mase and LA stepped out with black hoodies on as they walked up toward them.

"Yo Pillz, let me run. I got some business I need to take care of."

"Say less. You know where to find me at."

"Copy that." Blue dapped Pillz up before walking away.

Pillz turned around and saw LA and Mase walking up with their hands under their shirt.

"Yo Pillz, what the fuck is popping?"

"Everything is popping. What the fuck you talking about, LA?"

"I'm saying if I ain't eating, then you ain't eating. That's what the fuck I'm talking about, nigga."

"Nigga, what's that? A fucking threat? Suck my dick."

Mase pulled his gun out and looked at Pillz.

"Suck what? Pussy nigga, this is truth of the block. Now, you see what the fuck it is."

Pillz smiled then lowered his head and hurried up and pulled his gun out. "What the fuck you talking about? My heart don't pump Kool aid, nigga. I'm with all the fuck shit and I'm eating real good, broke babies."

"I like that tough guy shit. Just know what time it is the next time I pull up, doggy."

"I ain't ya doggy and both of ya can suck on an infected dick sideways. Pop nigga if it's in your heart." Mase tapped LA on the chest.

"Come on. We out see you soon, Pillz."

"No nigga. Don't see me. Next time I see you, shells are flying."

"Keep that promise, little nigga."

"Next time you pull up on the block, your people are going to have a picture of you on they T-shirts, looking down in a box at ya ass." Mase ain't say a word to him and LA got back in the SUV and pulled off.

"Mase, how are we going to deal with this pussy ass, disrespectful ass nigga, Pillz?"

"That nigga is dead. His eyes are still open. I would have popped his ass just now, but I don't know who he was talking to and that nigga saw our faces. I don't have time for a murder case, attorney, judges, DA's, court fees, bonds and all the other bullshit that comes with it. His time is coming. Then, we going to pop his ass. On gang."

SAYNOMORE

Chapter 46

"Pillz, you telling me that them niggas pulled up on the block talking crazy?"

"Yeah, Murder, shit is bananas right now. I'm running low on coffee. I'm out here by myself. You behind the wall facing crazy ass charges, A-Dog still in ICU in a fucking coma knocked out."

"Look, Pillz, I need you to be on your fucking A game and keep your eyes open. That pretty bitch is behind all of this. She been playing niggas from the jump. We been having so much hate in our hearts over how shit went down with Tray fucking with Don Killer that we been blind to how shit really was playing out. Look, there ain't no rainbow at the end of my tunnel. The crown is on your head till A-Dog come home. Look, this phone is about to hang up. Be safe out here, my nigga."

"I will. Keep your head up in there and I got you from out here, fam."

"Copy that." Pillz hung up the phone and looked around on the block, knowing Murder was right. He has to be smart. You can't get money and be blazing shots at the same time.

***

Tuggy was smoking a Black-n-Mild in the Pinks when KP pulled up. He watched as he got out the car and walked up on him.

"Yo Tuggy, you must think I'm pussy or sweet or something? Pulling up at my girl spot looking for me." Tuggy threw the Black-n-Mild down and got into KP face.

"No nigga I don't think you pussy. I think you are a whole bitch and a half nigga." KP pulled his gun out.

"What was you saying about that bitch and a half nigga?"

"Nigga my heart ain't pumping no fucking Kool aid because you holding nigga. You look even more like a bitch now then you did before. Now, blast nigga. Do what the fuck your heart is telling you to do and like I told your bitch; you better have that bread you owe me by the end of the week."

"Just know this is your lucky day. Next time you come to my people spot and I catch you down bad, bang motherfucker. When I get the bread, I'll pull up on you." Tuggy looked around at everyone in the apartment watching them.

"Oh, I see you are a gangster with a heart. Too many eyes around for you to get your hands dirty. Too many witnesses, baby boy?"

"I will see you soon, nigga. Just know that."

"I hope so, motherfucker." KP put his gun up and got back in his car and drove off. Tuggy just watched him leave.

***

"Shay, dog this shit is crazy. Them brown niggas and stick boys got the blocks on fire. One time is every fucking where fucking the money up."

"Just chill, son. Shit is going to pan out real soon. Look at it this way, the heat ain't on us so let them fools body each other and the boys in blue can clean them up." Dolow nodded and lit the blunt he had in his hand.

"I'm down with however you want to play this game out, big homie."

"Say less. You know how we rock. Now pass the fucking blunt, little nigga."

Chapter 47

Monay drove around Amityville in her black BMW. She rode down Overland Ave and pulled over when she saw Pillz leaving against his car, smoking a blunt. Pillz watched as Monay opened the car door and stepped out.

"You must be lost from the fuck shit you just pulled off."

"And here I thought you were about your paper, Pillz."

"I am, and I'm also about loyalty. Because you of you one of my homies is in ICU and the other one is looking at three life sentences plus eighty-five years. Now, you pulling up on the block like you can't get smoked."

"Motherfucker, I am loyal to my dead little sister who Trap and Murder killed. She wasn't even twenty-one years old yet. So yeah, I played them niggas. When you ask me where my loyalty is at, it's to my little sister that's six feet deep."

"I don't know about none of that shit. I just know what you did and how you played the game."

"So, if you feel that way, why ain't I dead yet?"

"We all have our reason for what we do. I can't judge a book by its cover. I just hope the shit you are saying is true."

"If you ain't think it was true, I think I would be dead already."

Pillz dropped his blunt and walked off, not looking back at Monay. Monay looked at Pillz before walking back to her car and driving off.

***

"Yeah, yeah. I told ya how shit was going to play out and ya dudes still pulled up on son. Now, ya got me looking crazy like I was on the fuck shit, LA."

Pillz watched from the side of the house as Shawn was talking on the phone. He watched as Shawn lowered his head to light his blunt. It was pitch black outside. Pillz pulled his gun out and waited for Shawn to turn around so he could run up on him without him seeing him.

"Yo LA, let me call you back. I'm about to make this money and smoke this gas fam." Shawn hung up the phone and turned around toward the streets.

Pillz ran up on him gun out. "What's up nigga?"

Shawn turned around to see Pillz pointing a gun at his face. He dropped his blunt and took a step back.

"Yo Pillz, what the fuck?"

"Yeah, nigga, you pull up on me about some work and not even a few hours go by before Mase and LA pull up on me, guns out."

"Homie, you tripping. I ain't have shit to do with that, on gang."

"Nigga you must think I'm sweet or something. So, it was just some kind of coincidence the same day just a few hours apart from each other. Nigga which one you working."

"Pillz, you know how I get down. That ain't even my fucking style." Shawn looked at Pillz as he had the gun to his face. Pillz had the look of death in his eyes as he looked at Shawn ready to kill him.

"Naw homie, I know how them stick niggas get down and you run with them niggas. Now if I found out you set me up, I'm going to push your shit back, nigga." Pillz lowered his gun and walked backwards to the side of the house, out of Shawn's eyesight.

***

KP walked up to Shay Dog as he was smoking a blunt in his car. He was sitting in his driveway listening to the sound system blast Jay-Z *The Black Album.*

"What's up, fam," KP said as he dapped Shay Dog up.

"Shit, just watching the block. I heard about that shit that went down with you and Tuggy the other day in the Pinks."

"Yeah, you know I pulled up on that fool all the way on the fuck shit. Strong press game."

"Yeah, I was told you pulled the hammer out on son to let him know what the fuck the business was."

"You already know how I give it up, big homie."

"Yeah, I do. That's why when I was told you pulled up then what happened, I was like why he ain't fire off in son shit?"

"Too many eyes was on the block. I would have been in the hotseat. Somebody would have dropped a dime on me if I would have flatlined him."

"If you know that, why you pull out on him in front of everybody out there?" Just to let niggas know you holding a tool?"

"I saw the fool and just pulled up on him."

"I feel you, but you already know how Tuggy gets down. The first chance he gets, he going to blaze your ass."

"I ain't worried about that soft ass nigga. If he want smoke, I'm set his ass on fire."

"Say less, homie. So, what's the word? What's your plans for today?"

"Shit, I'm about to find me a bitch to lay up with in the cut right now."

"Do you and pull up on me later, baby boy."

"Copy that, big bro." KP dapped Shay Dog up before walking off.

***

Pillz's phone went off. He looked and saw it was a collect call from Murder. He answered the phone and pressed the number 1 to accept the call.

"What's the word fam?"

"Shit, my attorney came to me talking crazy on some monkey ass banana ass shit."

"What he talking about?"

"Taking a plea for life without parole or I'm looking at the death sentence, fam."

"Beloved, what you going to do?"

"I have to take the plea. My attorney showed me the video of me bodying that fool Don Killer and talking about the police we wacked. Shit is crazy ugly on my end."

"Damn, my guy. I don't know what to say to you. You know I got your back out here, hands down. Bread on your books and all."

"I already be knowing, fam."

"Murder, let me tell you. That bitch Monay pulled up on me a few days ago, trying to talk to a nigga. I dubbed that shit all the way out."

"What the fuck? You should have bodied that bitch."

"Too many eyes, my nigga. I would have been in there with you on a murder rap."

"Copy, copy. I feel you but you know the first chance you get what to do."

"Already. Any word on A-Dog?"

"The homie still sleeping from what I was told."

"Damn, he's been out for about six months now."

"He's good. My homie is a real trooper. Look, this phone is about to hang up. Stay up fam and remember what I said homie."

"Already. I'm put that work in."

"I'll hit you up this week, fam."

"Copy that."

Chapter 48

"It's been six months since Don Killer been dead. This year just went sideways and in the end we found out it was Murder and A-Dog's pussy asses who bodied the homies." Homicide looked at everyone in the apartment as he smoked his blunt.

"The point I'm making is, we don't have shit. Them Browns niggas took over every fucking thing and flooded the blocks. We don't have no work or no plug. We all put blood in the streets Kane, except for you." Homicide got up and walked to Kane and passed him a black .45 Colt. "Look, little homie, the past is over with. Don Killer's dead, Rock is dead, Murder is locked up and A-Dog in a fucking coma laid up in the hospital, but Pillz is still on the block. So, the only question is are you ready for that one-eight-seven?"

"Fucking right. Where that nigga at?"

"Nine of out ten times if he's not on Overland Ave, he's on Smith Street. Pull up on that pussy and let the bullets open his chest up."

"Say less, I'm on it. That fool is about to make Fox Five head-line news." Homicide watched as Kane tucked the .45 in his waist and put his hoodie on and walked out the apartment.

"Yo Homicide, you think Kane going to take care of that business?"

"Apple, real talk, if he don't, then we are going to take care of his ass then."

"Bang-Bang, I'm down for whatever, Homicide."

"I already know."

***

Pillz was leaning against his car, watching the block as he made his plays, when Faith walked up to him.

"Da real Pillz burry. What's good?"

"Shit Faith, just watching out for these goofy ass niggas."

"What you mean?" Pillz looked at Faith and shook his head.

"Since shit went bananas with Murder and A-Dog, them niggas from the sticks pulled up on me."

"Who was it from the sticks?"

"Shawn with his weak ass game, and not even a few hours passed by, then Mase and LA pulled up with they pussy ass, talking sideways out the mouth."

"What they say? They trying to put the press game down on you? Like on some State Property shit."

"Like on some goofy ass shit. The only thing they ain't say was get down or lay down. Niggas was on some shit if they can't eat then nobody can eat on the block. Then, Mase pulled his gun out. So, I pulled out and told them fools we can all die today. LA said some funny ass shit then them niggas got in the truck and drove away."

"Real shit, them some clown ass dudes. Them bums just mad because without Trance or Rah, they broke."

"Big fucking facts." Faith watched as Kane walked up on them. "Yo Pillz, what's up?"

"Shit, just chopping it up with Faith. What's up?"

Faith looked at Kane and knew something wasn't right.

"Homicide ain't respecting how shit played out with Don Killer. Homie talking about a body for a body."

Pillz looked at Faith and when he turned around Kane was pulling out his .45. Faith grabbed his hand as he was pulling the gun out. Pillz punched him in the face, dropping him. Kane let the gun go. Faith picked it up and pulled the trigger, shooting Kane in the chest one time. Pillz ran to Faith and took the gun from her and looked down at Kane and shot him two more times in the chest, killing him.

"Faith, get up out of here before anybody see you. I don't need you wrapped up in a murder case, baby girl."

Faith looked at Pillz and ran off. Pillz turned around to see if anybody was watching him. He took his Browns flag out and wiped off the gun and dropped it off on Kane's dead body. He got into his car and drove off looking in the rearview mirror.

***

"Yo Homicide, Overland Ave is flooded with five-point-o right now."

"Kane put Pillz to bed?"

"That's not even the story that I got. I was told he got popped three times. Long story short, Kane dead, Homicide."

"So, Pillz think he's built like that."

"The fuck if I know. What you want to do, big bro?"

"We got to body this nigga and I want it loud. Just like when Trance and them police got rocked to bed. You remember how that shit hit the news waves? I want it just like that. I don't give a fuck how many people got to die because whoever is out there with him is the enemy.

"Well, you know he's going to be laying low for a minute."

"I don't give a fuck. Flush him out."

"Copy copy. I'm about to go play the block and see what the streets is talking about, fam."

"Say less."

***

Pillz pulled up behind the brick house. He jumped out of his car and was looking before he started talking to himself.

"What the fuck man? I know I just ain't flatline that duck ass boy in front of Faith. What the fuck was I thinking?" These niggas have a red dot on my back. My luck can't be this bad. I didn't step on no crack or walk over no open grave. I know it was that pussy nigga, Homicide who sent that boy at me. I'll show them who they fucking with, on Browns. It's shoot or get shot now. Black Timbs and black hoodies. It's murder season on da gang." Pillz jumped back into his car and drove off with 50 Cent's *Many Men* playing.

SAYNOMORE

Chapter 49

Murder sat at the table when the alarm went off. He looked around the dining hall and saw an officer running and teargas being shot out of guns. Inmates were fighting with officers. Murder saw two police officers running his way. He picked up his food tray and smacked one of the COs in the face with it. He punched the other CO in the face and ran out of the dining hall and watched as hell was breaking loose at the prison. He took off running down the walk with other inmates who was trying to hop the gate. Murder jumped on the gate and was stabbed three times in the back. He let go of the gate and fell on his back. When he looked up, someone with a mask on stabbed him over and over again in the chest and took off running. Murder looked at him as he ran off before he closed his eyes, taking his last breath.

***

Monay sat down on her loveseat as she watched the news. The news story was on the prison riot and how a number of officers were hurt. Two of them were in the ICU, one inmate dead and three other inmates in ICU as well. She took a sip of her tea when she saw Murder's picture on the TV screen as the inmate who was killed during the prison riot before cutting her TV off and walking up the stairs to her bedroom. One thing Omar always told her was to always conceal your intentions and to keep people off balance and to always keep your hands clean. Murder was still a threat, and she knew that but for the right price anybody can be killed no matter the place or time. Murder death was proof of that.

***

Homicide walked up to the dice game on Smith Street.

"Yo, how much is in the pot?"

"Twelve hundred right now. Side bets fifty dollars, baby boy," Mike-B said.

"So, you running the bank?"

"It's big money over here, real talk. Drop your bet or stand back."

"Nigga you ain't saying shit. Drop your money or stand back? How about this, I'ma match what's in the pot." Homicide dropped $1,200 on the ground. "Let's see what the fuck you talking about with your roll game."

"You ain't saying shit but a word, my guy."

"Mike-B rolled the dice. Everyone watched as it hit the wall at the Pinks. "Head crack niggas what the fuck ya talking about. Pay me. Pay me, I want my check now."

"That lucky ass shit."

"I don't give a fuck, pay me. How that wack ass commercial go? It's my money and I want it now so pay the fuck up."

"You got it, player. I don't want no smoke."

"What's up, Homicide? You trying to bet again on the roll?"

"No, I was really looking for that boy, Pillz. I thought he might be out here."

"Naw, son is on Avon posted up."

"You sure about that?"

"Yeah, facts but I'm about to roll these dice fam and get back to this money."

"Stay up, fam. I'll get at you later."

"Copy that my guy."

Homicide walked off with his hoodie on headed to Avon.

***

"Faith, shit is foul right now. When I heard that fucked up news, ain't no way I wanted to believe it but when I saw son face on the news that shit put a hole in my heart. Me and son didn't fuck with each other like that. He got locked up. A-Dog is going to be sick hands down."

"Pillz, A-Dog is good right now. You need to think about yourself. Someone just tried to clap you not even five days ago. The block know you are the only one holding weight right now. Niggas is hungry out here and real talk you are the prey right now."

"Real talk, Faith. Motherfuckers ain't happy until their face is on a nigga T-shirt."

"Look Pillz, just be safe out here. I have to go make some plays."

"Yo Faith, you all in one, baby girl. You are a dime piece, a trap queen, a shooter."

"I have to be because a bitch like me ain't going out bad," Faith said that with a smile on her face as she got into her car and drove off. Pillz lit his blunt up, still posted on the block. He saw Robin walking his way.

"Hey Pillz, you have a twenty on you?"

"Yeah, I got you Robin. How the fuck you been?"

"Good, why you way over here now and not on Smith Street? This is a long ass walk."

"Shit is crazy over there right now so I'm just playing the cut for right now until shit cool down."

"Okay, at least I know where to find you at now."

"That's a true story. I'ma be out here for a few more hours."

"Okay, I'll send word out there where to find you at."

"Do that, Robin."

Robin took the 20 crack rocks in her hand and walked through the path.

"Yo Pillz, what's up nigga?"

"Whatever the fuck you talking about nigga!" Pillz pulled his gun out and looked at Homicide.

Homicide was smoking a Black-n-Mild when Pillz pulled his gun out on him.

"I see you packing the heat right now. What you going to blast, nigga?"

"If you don't get the fuck off my block, I'ma put another body on this bitch."

"You must think you are the only one holding. You so focused on me you ain't even looking around."

Pillz looked to the right and saw three more niggas walking up with guns out. Without saying a word, he pointed his gun at Homicide and shot three times and took off running. Homicide body hit the ground. His boys started to shoot at Pillz as he was running behind the house. Pillz jumped two gates and got in his car. He had parked two blocks over and drove off. Apple just looked at Homicide's lifeless body and took off running.

Chapter 50

Pillz walked into Fat-Tee's house on Albany Ave. Fat-Tee looked at him when he walked into the door. Fat-Tee had his gun in his hand looking at Pillz.

"Yo, if it ain't America's most wanted in the hood. Come in, hot boy. Wait, you are already in my house. Close my front door."

Pillz dapped Fat-Tee up then took a seat at the table.

"Tee, shit is crazy right now. Homicide pulled up on me. I had to pop son and his niggas."

"I heard that shit. You should have been pulled up on me, doggy."

"I'm here now, fam."

"Check me out. You know the streets are talking so I'll pull up on them niggas for you. Just stay ducked off right now until you hear from me."

"Copy that, beloved. I just need this nightmare to be over." Pillz dapped Fat-Tee up before he walked out the door.

"Yo, Pillz, shoot or get shot." Pillz looked at Fat-Tee.

"Porsha life." Fat-Tee watched as Pillz walked out the door through the path to the Flattops.

***

Fat-Tee stepped out of his 2021 Charger and walked up to the white house on Great Neck Road right off of Miller Avenue. He looked around to see a few people on the block, walked up to the front door and knocked two times.

"Yo, who is it?"

"Fat-Tee," Fat-Tee just listened as the door was being unlocked. Apple opened the door

"So, you at my door? You must be here on some peace treaty shit."

"Are you going to let me in, or do I have to stand right here?" Apple looked at Fat-Tee and cut his eyes.

"You good, come in."

Fat-Tee walked past Apple and looked at his two homies in the living room, smoking a blunt and playing 2K live.

"You came by here, so what the fuck is on your mind?"

"This shit about you and Pillz. How many more bodies have to drop before this shit is over with?"

"Why the fuck you care?"

"Don Killer is dead, and Murder is dead; Homicide is dead. This beef needs to be fucking deaded, Apple."

"Nigga you act like you are in the fucking streets. When was the last time you put a body on your gun? You pulling up on me with this boy scout shit. What happened to die and not cry. Shoot or get shot. Kill and not care."

"Apple, you know who the fuck I am. I don't have to play the block. I am the fucking block and like I said, this beef shit needs to be fucking deaded."

"Nigga this shit will be fucking deaded when I'm in a fucking box. You can take that to the fucking heart, nigga."

"Yeah, I think I'll do that Apple and take it to the fucking heart." Fat-Tee pulled his gun out, grabbed Apple, put his gun to his head and pulled the trigger twice as held his body up. Fat-Tee let him go and watched as his body hit the floor. He then stood up over top of him and shot him three more times in the head before looking at Apple's homies in the living room.

"Like I said, this beef shit is over with or do I still have to make my point and put another body on my gun?"

"Naw, you good, fam. You made your point."

"I'm glad you see it from my point of view now. Take care of this nigga body. Drop it off in the dance or somewhere out of the Ville." Fat-Tee kicked Apple's body as he walked out of the house.

***

"Shay Dog, niggas is dropping like flies out here. Niggas is trying to make Amityville number one murder capital of the world. This shit is wild. The block is hot."

"I be knowing, little homie. This shit ain't good for nobody. Jump out boys running up patting niggas down, and it ain't no fucking better that Homicide got killed and the next fucking day Apple gets rocked to sleep and dumped off on a straight path, KP."

214

"Word is Pillz caught them bodies."

"I can go for Homicide but Pillz ain't the type to carry a body somewhere and dump if off. I'm not saying he ain't built like that. I just don't see him doing no shit like that."

"I just hope all this shit is over with so I can go back to chasing this money. My pockets is about to be on E, real shit and if I can't get it on the block, the next step for me is running up in a nigga house and putting the 9 in his mouth."

"Just chill, cowboy. Ain't nothing forever. This shit is going to blow over real soon and niggas is going to get back to making they bread. Just fall back in the cut for now."

"Copy that."

SAYNOMORE

Chapter 51

Monay pulled up on Faith as she was walking down Overland Ave. Faith looked at the white G-Wagon as it pulled over in front of her and watched as Monay stepped out of the truck.

"Excuse me, do you know Pillz?" Monay asked.

"Yeah, I do and who are you?" Monay looked at Faith and could tell she worked the block as a trap girl. She saw the baby 9mm faith was trying to duck off under her shirt.

"I'm Monay. Pillz know who I am, and you are?"

"Faith. If he know you, why don't you just call him?"

"We don't have that type of relationship yet. It's more like when I see you, I see you."

"I hear you. When I see him, I'll tell him you were looking for him, Monay."

"Thanks. Let me get you something for your troubles."

Monay walked to her G-Wagon and pulled out a paper bag. Faith watched as she walked back to her with the bag in her hand.

"Here, this is for you."

"What is it?"

"Let's just call it a gift out of respect for girls like us."

Monay smiled as she handed her the bag and walked back to her G-Wagon. It was only seven grams of coke. It was for Pillz now. It's a blessing for someone else but she was sure Pillz would get the picture. Faith looked into the paper bag and saw the cocaine and the back of Monay G-Wagon as she was pulling off. She put the bag inside of her coat and walked off.

***

Pillz pulled up in front of Faith's spot and got out of his car. Faith was sitting down on the steps, smoking a blunt.

"Faith, what's up, baby girl? I got your text. What's good?"

"This fly ass bitch pulled up looking for you today. She said her name was Monay. She was here like two hours ago."

"Monay. She say what she wanted?"

"No but she was iced up like she was getting ready for a Future video."

"Who was she with?"

"No one. She was dolow pushing a white G-Wagon and she blessed me with pure cocaine."

"Faith, that bitch is a whole rated R TV story."

"That's why you ain't fucking with her?"

"No, it's more to it. For me to tell you the story behind the scenes, it's going to take today and tomorrow with no pauses, but long story short, Don-Killer had her baby sister bodied and that's when the bottle popped."

"So, why she pulling up on you now?"

"She know I wasn't a part of that shit, and I was just fucking with them for the dollar. Real talk, the streets don't love nobody, and niggas say they loyal to you, but they real loyalty is to what you can do for them, not you. So, I'm loyal to them niggas the same way they are loyal to me to see what I can get out of them."

"For real, for real, I respect that Pillz. So, what you going to do about her?"

"I don't know yet, Faith."

"She might be the plug you need. She might be your come up."

"Or my downfall. Now, relight that blunt and pass it."

"You can relight the blunt. I'm about to go cook this coke baby girl gave me. I just ain't want to talk over the phone. That's why I asked you to come over."

"I got you Faith. I'll pull up on you later, ma."

"Cool."

***

Mase sat on the hood of his car drinking an orange Fanta and smoking a Black-n-Mild as he watched 5.0 drive pass his spot. Amityville was hot. The blocks was empty. You had police on Albany Ave. and Smith Street. They were in the Flattops. They was on Great Neck Rd, 110 and Bay View. LA and Shawn was ducked off. It was two sweeps in the last week. They were looking for someone to put the bodies on, but nobody would talk. Mase got off the hood of his car when he saw Monay ride pass in her G-Wagon. By the time he made it to the corner, she was gone. When he turned back around, he saw the police pulling up on him.

"Fuck," he watched as they got out of the car and walked up on him.

"Put your hands where I can see them."

"Man, what the fuck you want? You just saw me sitting on the hood of my car in the driveway."

"I ain't ask you to speak. I said put your hands where I can see them."

The other officer looked at him with his hand on his gun. "Now sir, do as you were told to do."

Mase placed his hands on the top of his head as the officers walked up to him.

"Do you have anything on you that we need to know about?"

"No." Mase had a nasty look on his face as he was getting patted down.

"He's clean, Mark."

"Let me tell you now. There is no posting up on the blocks, no hanging out. Next time I catch you on the corner, you are going for a ride to the Fifth Precinct.

Mase ain't say a word. He just walked back to his house and closed his front gate behind him. Salt and Pepper were two fuck police officers in the hood and Mase couldn't wait to kill one of their asses if not both of them. Mase's phone went off. He looked and saw it was LA calling him.

"Yo, what's good, fam?"

"Shit, over here on Overland waiting for that boy Pillz to come through. He's going to come off that work or lay the fuck down. I don't care how the fuck it go."

"Leave that shit alone. The block is hot. Five-o everywhere. Them clowns just jumped out on me not even five minutes ago."

"Mase, this is the only way right now."

"LA, if them boys catch you, they might try and charge you with all them bodies. While your ass is sitting on death row, Pillz is still going to be on the block."

"Say less. I'm about to pull up on you now."

"Copy that."

***

Fat-Tee pulled up in front of Pillz spot, smoking a blunt. Pillz looked out of the front window as Fat-Tee walked up to the front door. Pillz opened the door for him.

"What's rocking, fam?"

"Niggas like us. Who's in the spot with you?"

"Me, myself and I. I'm on some dolow shit until I know who is who. I don't have time to get rocked to sleep."

"I hear you. I took care of that nigga, Apple. He wasn't trying to hear what I was trying to say so I let the four pound do the rest of the talking."

"I already knew what time it was when you pulled up. You don't do no negotiation you fall in line or get your chest knocked off." Both of them started to laugh.

"Hands down, my guy."

"So, what's the move now?"

"Shit, I'm about to get back to my spot. The block is hot right now and I ain't got time to talk with the po po."

"Respect, fam."

"Always. Just know I'ma be calling in a favor so be on call."

"Already." Pillz watched as Fat-Tee walked out of his house back to his car and drove off.

Chapter 52

"Faith, I feel like I done looked the devil's demon in the eyes, challenged death and walked through hell. It's like a nigga put a brick on my head and got the whole hood looking for my ass. Every time I turn around, I feel there is some more bullshit in the air."

"Real shit Pillz, you need to think about where your loyalty lies because all I see that A-Dog and Murder did for you was put you in warfare with niggas from the 40s, Sticks, and Flattops. Don't end up with an ID number or end up on someone T-shirt trying to stay loyal to some niggas who don't give a fuck about you."

"And why you say that?"

"Because you said it first. They only fuck with you because what you can do for them."

"Real shit, I just hope all of this is over with now. I'm shell shocked. I don't want niggas around me. I can't stand this goofy ass shit."

"You get goofy ass shit when you fucking with goofy ass niggas, Pillz."

"Dead ass, you are right. I'm about to head to the spot. I'll link up with you tomorrow."

"You know where I am at."

Monay sat in her black BMW on the corner and watched as Pillz left Faith's house in his car. Once he was gone, she pulled up in front of Faith's house. She was going to follow him but instead she said to herself she would deal with Faith. Pillz loyalty was with his team, and she respected that but she also knew in time he would see their true face behind the mask. Only then, Pillz would know their loyalty was fake.

Faith looked out of her window and saw the black BMW in front of her house. She stepped out of the door. Monay stepped out of the car.

"I see you working the block late."

"No, I just saw your car in front of my spot and I wanted to see who car it was. Now, I know. Was you watching my house?"

"No, I was just riding by and stopped when I saw Pillz car but I'm not going to chase no man to become rich. I'm already up."

"What happened with you and Murder?"

"Let's just say I saw through his fake mask when everyone else thought it was his face. I was going to kill him no matter what once I learned he had my sister's blood on his hands. Him and Don Killer. You kill my cat I kill your dogs."

"So, you had Murder killed?"

"Let's just say everyone have a date and his time was up."

"I respect that. So, let me ask you this. Can I reup with you?"

"Always. How much you want?"

"Let me count up my coins and I'll let you know."

"Faith, take my number and call me when you are ready to do business."

"I got you, Monay."

"That's good to hear. I'll see you later then, Faith."

"I'll call you in a day or two."

"I'll be waiting." Monay got into her car and drove off as Faith walked back into her house.

***

A-Dog opened his eyes and looked around the hospital room. His mouth was very dry, and he felt weak. His right hand was cuffed to the bed. His mind was blank, and he didn't remember nothing. He didn't know how long he had been in the hospital for. A few minutes passed when the nurse walked into the room.

"Adam, I see that you are up. How do you feel?"

"Lost, weak, thirsty. How long have I been here for?"

The nurse was looking at his chart. "Friday will be one year. Do you remember anything?"

"No."

"Let me go get the doctor. He needs to know that you are up," A-Dog laid his head back down on the pillow and closed his eyes. He tried to think about the last thing he could remember. He opened his eyes when he heard the room door open back up. He looked up and saw two police officers walk in the door with the doctor.

"Weak, thirsty."

"Well, we will give you something to drink in a minute. You have been in a coma for a year now. You hit your head pretty hard. Do you remember how you got here?"

"No, I don't remember anything at all."

"Well, you were in a bad car accident where the car flipped over three times. You are lucky to be alive."

"Why am I handcuffed and what are they doing here?"

"We are here because you are facing criminal charges and when the doctor discharges you, you are coming with us to the fifth precinct?"

"Officers, I would like to keep him here a few more days just to watch him. No more than 72 hours."

"You hear that, Adam? Three more days of this luxury hospital for you."

A-Dog just laid his head down as he tried to wrap his head around everything.

***

Monay blessed Faith with a half of bird for $15,000 up front and $8,000 on the back end. Faith was in her house cooking up when she heard a knock at her door. She grabbed her gun and walked to the front door.

"Who is it?"

"Pillz, Faith."

Faith opened the door and looked at Pillz.

"Come in my nigga."

"What you got going on in here."

"Just trying to flip my dollars, cooking up this work."

"Put in that work. I see you popping big shit." Pillz was looking at the work Faith had in the kitchen on the table.

"Who fucked with you on the re-up?"

"Monay gave me a player price on a half of bird."

"Wait, you are telling me that you are rocking with her now?"

"It's nothing like that. It's all business and the money is pleasure on my end."

"I ain't fucking with her but I ain't mad at you. You saw an open door and went through that shit. I respect the game. So what, you selling weight now?"

"I'll sell a few ounces. Once I cut it two or three times, then I'ma play the block. It's trap season."

"I see you, homie. Shit, I'm about to roll out and let you get your trap on. The block is dry, so all the baby love is going to come your way." Faith smiled.

"I already know, Pillz."

Pillz walked up to Faith and gave her a hug before walking out the house. As Pillz pulled off, he saw Black King pull up and walk into Faith's spot. Black King was a foul ass nigga, a snake in the grass, a nigga who would sell fake rocks in the hood, fucking up the money for the real niggas on the block. In a nutshell, dude is real bad news. Pillz told himself he was going to tell Faith watch the company she kept.

"What's up, Black King?" Faith greeted.

"Shit, Shay Dog told me you had that pure cocaine on deck. How much you letting the twenty-eight grams go for?"

"It's tax season. I'm cracking heads for eighteen hundred on the ounce. You good with that?"

"Yeah, facts. Let me see what it looks like?"

"Cool, let me get that for you."

Black King watched as Faith pulled out the half of brick she flipped twice. He walked to the table and pick it up. "Yeah, Faith that's that butter. I can work with this. Let me get two for the thirty-five hundred."

"I can do that, Black King." When Faith turned around, Black King pulled out his .45 and pointed it at her head.

"Matter of fact, let me get all that off your hands." Faith looked at the gun Black King had pointed at her.

"Nigga, you got to be fucking kidding me. Coming in my spot with all this goofy as shit."

"You better hurry the fuck up before I push your wig back, bitch."

Faith looked at Black King with hate in her eyes as she put the work in her bag.

"Faith don't take this to the heart. You was just an easy lick. It was a come up for me. You just caught the bad end of the stick today."

"I'll see you soon, Black King. You can flip a coin on that promise."

"I know you tough and got the heart of a lion that's why I'm end this shit now." Black King looked at Faith and pulled the trigger three times, taking the breath out of her body as the bullets ripped through her chest, claiming her life. Black King looked as her lifeless body laid in a pool of blood. He picked up the bag with the cocaine in it and walked out the house.

SAYNOMORE

Chapter 53

Pillz walked out the house and looked down the street at the police in front of Faith house. The street was blocked off. He walked down the block to see what was going on.

"Yo, what the fuck is going on down here? They raided Faith spot, Blue?"

"Hell no, Pillz. You ain't hear the news? Faith got bodied last night. Shot three times in her chest. Her mother found her dead this morning."

"Don't tell me no shit like that, Blue."

"True story, homie. Shit sad."

"I got to push off. I got to take care of some shit, Blue."

"Pillz, you good, homie?"

"Fuck no. I'm out." Pillz walked off with his hand on his gun. His mind was made up. He knew Black King killed his homie. Whoever Black King was with when he pulled up on him was dead too. All them niggas was going to be in a black bag, guilty by association and he put that on the gang. Pillz got in his car and drove off, thinking about Faith and how close he was to her.

***

"Nigga you really bodied that bitch, King?"

"Fucking right. Now, we got a brick and a half from that dead bitch."

"Shit that was the move now. We just need to know who that bitch plug is so we can keep it coming in."

"Fucking right." Pillz put his hoodie on and his Browns flag over his face. AT already dropped a dime on where Black King was at, and she told him he wasn't alone. Pillz put the thirty two clip in the Mack-11 and stepped out of his car. He looked around the block to see who was out. The way he felt, the Judge and DA could have been walking down the block and shit still was about to do down. Pillz closed his eyes before he kicked the door in.

"Bang Bang, motherfucker. I know you ain't think shit was that sweet, pussy." Pillz let off his Mack-11, shooting everyone he saw. Black King was laying on the floor holding his shoulder where he was shot at. Pillz looked to the left where he saw the two niggas dead who took head shots. "Nigga what the fuck you thought this was going to be a happy ending story?" You got me fucked up. Faith ain't going to die alone pussy."

"Nigga, fuck that bitch." Black King looked at Pillz as he pulled the trigger and sparks flew from the Mack-11 spitting bullets out, hitting him in the face, killing him. Pillz looked at the kilo and a half on the floor that fell through the glass table in the living room. He thought about Faith and left it there. If she couldn't have it, no-body would. He walked out of the house back to his car. As he pulled off, the police were coming down the street.

Chapter 54

A-Dog looked around the courtroom at everyone sitting down. His attorney was talking to him on his behalf of the pleas he was about to take. His attorney stopped talking when the Judge started

"Mr. Mason, are you pleading guilty at your own free will today?"

"Yes, your Honor, I am."

"Have you been threatened to plead guilty by anybody?

"No, I haven't, your Honor."

"Then, within the power of this court, I hereby sentence you to a term of five years in prison for possession of a firearm and obstruction of justice to be ran concurrent with each other for a term of no more than five years in the NYC justice system."

A-Dog looked at his attorney and shook his hand as he walked out of the courtroom.

A-Dog hadn't been out of the hospital three weeks and was already on his way up North to prison. He really ain't give a fuck about the time. His loyalty was to Murder and Murder's loyalty to him. Murder took responsibility for everything to free him up over the last year. One thing he can say is Murder lived by the number one street rule; death before dishonor. Murder still had his loyalty in his grave. Blood ain't make them related, loyalty made them related, and trust made them brothers.

***

Pillz sat on the steps with his hands on his gun. His head was down, and the beck of his gun rested on his forehead as tears dropped from his eyes on the steps. He thought about Faith. Deep in his heart, he knew he should have gone back when he saw Black King walking into her spot. Killing Black King ain't make him feel better. Street justice was the best justice and watching Black King take his last breath was the sun coming out after the rainstorm for him. Faith broke the rules of the streets. Never sell drugs where you rest at, and never let nobody know your next move. For breaking them rules, she paid the ultimate price with her life. Black King paid the ultimate price as well with his life. Everybody knows never fuck with a bitch yelling Brown. Albany Ave. and Smith Street was Pillz stomping ground. And Black King witnessed it firsthand when the bullets ran out with nasty sounds that took the breath out of his body, claiming his life. Everybody in Amityville knows Nika's and uptowns, stomp the ground, buggie down Browns. Smith Street Gang.

To Be Continued...
Gorillaz in the Trenches 2
Coming Soon

Lock Down Publications and Ca$h Presents assisted
publishing packages.

BASIC PACKAGE $499
Editing
Cover Design
Formatting

UPGRADED PACKAGE $800
Typing
Editing
Cover Design
Formatting

ADVANCE PACKAGE $1,200
Typing
Editing
Cover Design
Formatting
Copyright registration
Proofreading
Upload book to Amazon

LDP SUPREME PACKAGE $1,500
Typing
Editing
Cover Design
Formatting
Copyright registration
Proofreading
Set up Amazon account
Upload book to Amazon
Advertise on LDP Amazon and Facebook page

***Other services available upon request. Additional charges may apply
Lock Down Publications
P.O. Box 944
Stockbridge, GA 30281-9998
Phone # 470 303-9761

Submission Guideline

Submit the first three chapters of your completed manuscript to ldpsubmissions@gmail.com, subject line: Your book's title. The manuscript must be in a .doc file and sent as an attachment. Document should be in Times New Roman, double spaced and in size 12 font. Also, provide your synopsis and full contact information. If sending multiple submissions, they must each be in a separate email.

Have a story but no way to send it electronically? You can still submit to LDP/Ca$h Presents. Send in the first three chapters, written or typed, of your completed manuscript to:

LDP: Submissions Dept
Po Box 944
Stockbridge, Ga 30281

DO NOT send original manuscript. Must be a duplicate.

Provide your synopsis and a cover letter containing your full contact information.

Thanks for considering LDP and Ca$h Presents.

NEW RELEASES

THE STREETS NEVER LET GO 3 by ROBERT BAPTISTE

RICH $AVAGE 2 by MARTELL "TROUBLESOME" BOL-
DEN

A GANGSTA'S PARADISE by TRAI'QUAN

THE MURDER QUEENS 2 by MICHAEL GALLON

FOREVER GANGSTA 2 by ADRIAN DULAN

GORILLAZ IN THE TRENCHES by SAYNOMORE

SAYNOMORE

STRAIGHT BEAST MODE III

De'Kari

KINGPIN KILLAZ IV

STREET KINGS III

PAID IN BLOOD III

CARTEL KILLAZ IV

DOPE GODS III

Hood Rich

SINS OF A HUSTLA II

ASAD

RICH $AVAGE III

By Martell Troublesome Bolden

YAYO V

Bred In The Game 2

S. Allen

THE STREETS WILL TALK II

By Yolanda Moore

SON OF A DOPE FIEND III

HEAVEN GOT A GHETTO II

SKI MASK MONEY II

By Renta

LOYALTY AIN'T PROMISED III

By Keith Williams

I'M NOTHING WITHOUT HIS LOVE II

SINS OF A THUG II

TO THE THUG I LOVED BEFORE II

IN A HUSTLER I TRUST II

By Monet Dragun

QUIET MONEY IV

Gorillaz in the Trenches

EXTENDED CLIP III

THUG LIFE IV

By **Trai'Quan**

THE STREETS MADE ME IV

By **Larry D. Wright**

IF YOU CROSS ME ONCE II

ANGEL IV

By **Anthony Fields**

THE STREETS WILL NEVER CLOSE IV

By **K'ajji**

HARD AND RUTHLESS III

KILLA KOUNTY III

By **Khufu**

MONEY GAME III

By **Smoove Dolla**

JACK BOYS VS DOPE BOYS II

A GANGSTA'S QUR'AN V

COKE GIRLZ II

COKE BOYS II

By **Romell Tukes**

MURDA WAS THE CASE II

Elijah R. Freeman

THE STREETS NEVER LET GO III

By **Robert Baptiste**

AN UNFORESEEN LOVE IV

By **Meesha**

KING OF THE TRENCHES III
by **GHOST & TRANAY ADAMS**

MONEY MAFIA II

By **Jibril Williams**

237

SAYNOMORE

Gorillaz in the Trenches

By Corey Robinson
IT'S JUST ME AND YOU II
By Ah'Million
BORN IN THE GRAVE II
By Self Made Tay
FOREVER GANGSTA III
By Adrian Dulan
GORILLAZ IN THE TRENCHES II
By SayNoMore

Available Now

RESTRAINING ORDER **I & II**
By **CA$H & Coffee**
LOVE KNOWS NO BOUNDARIES **I II & III**
By **Coffee**
RAISED AS A GOON I, II, III & IV
BRED BY THE SLUMS I, II, III
BLAST FOR ME I & II
ROTTEN TO THE CORE I II III
A BRONX TALE I, II, III
DUFFLE BAG CARTEL I II III IV V VI
HEARTLESS GOON I II III IV V
A SAVAGE DOPEBOY I II

SAYNOMORE

DRUG LORDS I II III

CUTTHROAT MAFIA I II

KING OF THE TRENCHES

By **Ghost**

LAY IT DOWN **I & II**

LAST OF A DYING BREED I II

BLOOD STAINS OF A SHOTTA I & II III

By **Jamaica**

LOYAL TO THE GAME I II III

LIFE OF SIN I, II III

By **TJ & Jelissa**

BLOODY COMMAS I & II

SKI MASK CARTEL I II & III

KING OF NEW YORK I II,III IV V

RISE TO POWER I II III

COKE KINGS I II III IV V

BORN HEARTLESS I II III IV

KING OF THE TRAP I II

By **T.J. Edwards**

IF LOVING HIM IS WRONG…I & II

LOVE ME EVEN WHEN IT HURTS I II III

By **Jelissa**

WHEN THE STREETS CLAP BACK I & II III

THE HEART OF A SAVAGE I II III IV

MONEY MAFIA

LOYAL TO THE SOIL I II III

By **Jibril Williams**

A DISTINGUISHED THUG STOLE MY HEART I II & III

LOVE SHOULDN'T HURT I II III IV

240

Gorillaz in the Trenches

RENEGADE BOYS I II III IV

PAID IN KARMA I II III

SAVAGE STORMS I II III

AN UNFORESEEN LOVE I II III

By **Meesha**

A GANGSTER'S CODE I &, II III

A GANGSTER'S SYN I II III

THE SAVAGE LIFE I II III

CHAINED TO THE STREETS I II III

BLOOD ON THE MONEY I II III

A GANGSTA'S PAIN I II

By J-Blunt

PUSH IT TO THE LIMIT

By **Bre' Hayes**

BLOOD OF A BOSS **I, II, III, IV, V**

SHADOWS OF THE GAME

TRAP BASTARD

By **Askari**

THE STREETS BLEED MURDER **I, II & III**

THE HEART OF A GANGSTA I II& III

By **Jerry Jackson**

CUM FOR ME I II III IV V VI VII VIII

An **LDP Erotica Collaboration**

BRIDE OF A HUSTLA **I II & II**

THE FETTI GIRLS **I, II& III**

CORRUPTED BY A GANGSTA I, II III, IV

BLINDED BY HIS LOVE

THE PRICE YOU PAY FOR LOVE I, II ,III

DOPE GIRL MAGIC I II III

By **Destiny Skai**

SAYNOMORE

WHEN A GOOD GIRL GOES BAD
By **Adrienne**
THE COST OF LOYALTY I II III
By Kweli
A GANGSTER'S REVENGE **I II III & IV**
THE BOSS MAN'S DAUGHTERS I II III IV V
A SAVAGE LOVE **I & II**
BAE BELONGS TO ME I II
A HUSTLER'S DECEIT I, II, III
WHAT BAD BITCHES DO I, II, III
SOUL OF A MONSTER I II III
KILL ZONE
A DOPE BOY'S QUEEN I II III
TIL DEATH
By **Aryanna**
A KINGPIN'S AMBITON
A KINGPIN'S AMBITION **II**
I MURDER FOR THE DOUGH
By **Ambitious**
TRUE SAVAGE I II III IV V VI VII
DOPE BOY MAGIC I, II, III
MIDNIGHT CARTEL I II III
CITY OF KINGZ I II
NIGHTMARE ON SILENT AVE
THE PLUG OF LIL MEXICO II
CLASSIC CITY
By **Chris Green**
A DOPEBOY'S PRAYER
By **Eddie "Wolf" Lee**

Gorillaz in the Trenches

THE KING CARTEL **I, II & III**

By **Frank Gresham**

THESE NIGGAS AIN'T LOYAL **I, II & III**

By **Nikki Tee**

GANGSTA SHYT **I II &III**

By **CATO**

THE ULTIMATE BETRAYAL

By **Phoenix**

BOSS'N UP **I , II & III**

By **Royal Nicole**

I LOVE YOU TO DEATH

By **Destiny J**

I RIDE FOR MY HITTA

I STILL RIDE FOR MY HITTA

By **Misty Holt**

LOVE & CHASIN' PAPER

By **Qay Crockett**

TO DIE IN VAIN

SINS OF A HUSTLA

By **ASAD**

BROOKLYN HUSTLAZ

By **Boogsy Morina**

BROOKLYN ON LOCK I & II

By **Sonovia**

GANGSTA CITY

By **Teddy Duke**

A DRUG KING AND HIS DIAMOND I & II III

A DOPEMAN'S RICHES

HER MAN, MINE'S TOO I, II

CASH MONEY HO'S

SAYNOMORE

THE WIFEY I USED TO BE I II
PRETTY GIRLS DO NASTY THINGS
By Nicole Goosby
TRAPHOUSE KING **I II & III**
KINGPIN KILLAZ I II III
STREET KINGS I II
PAID IN BLOOD **I II**
CARTEL KILLAZ I II III
DOPE GODS I II
By **Hood Rich**
LIPSTICK KILLAH **I, II, III**
CRIME OF PASSION I II & III
FRIEND OR FOE I II III
By **Mimi**
STEADY MOBBN' **I, II, III**
THE STREETS STAINED MY SOUL I II III
By **Marcellus Allen**
WHO SHOT YA **I, II, III**
SON OF A DOPE FIEND I II
HEAVEN GOT A GHETTO
SKI MASK MONEY
Renta
GORILLAZ IN THE BAY **I II III IV**
TEARS OF A GANGSTA I II
3X KRAZY I II
STRAIGHT BEAST MODE I II
DE'KARI
TRIGGADALE I II III
MURDAROBER WAS THE CASE

Gorillaz in the Trenches

Elijah R. Freeman
GOD BLESS THE TRAPPERS I, II, III
THESE SCANDALOUS STREETS I, II, III
FEAR MY GANGSTA I, II, III IV, V
THESE STREETS DON'T LOVE NOBODY I, II
BURY ME A G I, II, III, IV, V
A GANGSTA'S EMPIRE I, II, III, IV
THE DOPEMAN'S BODYGAURD I II
THE REALEST KILLAZ I II III
THE LAST OF THE OGS I II III
Tranay Adams
THE STREETS ARE CALLING
Duquie Wilson
MARRIED TO A BOSS I II III
By Destiny Skai & Chris Green
KINGZ OF THE GAME I II III IV V VI
Playa Ray
SLAUGHTER GANG I II III
RUTHLESS HEART I II III
By Willie Slaughter
FUK SHYT
By Blakk Diamond
DON'T F#CK WITH MY HEART I II
By Linnea
ADDICTED TO THE DRAMA I II III
IN THE ARM OF HIS BOSS II
By Jamila
YAYO I II III IV
A SHOOTER'S AMBITION I II
BRED IN THE GAME

SAYNOMORE

By S. Allen
TRAP GOD I II III
RICH $AVAGE I II
MONEY IN THE GRAVE I II III
By Martell Troublesome Bolden
FOREVER GANGSTA I II
GLOCKS ON SATIN SHEETS I II
By Adrian Dulan
TOE TAGZ I II III IV
LEVELS TO THIS SHYT I II
IT'S JUST ME AND YOU
By Ah'Million
KINGPIN DREAMS I II III
RAN OFF ON DA PLUG
By Paper Boi Rari
CONFESSIONS OF A GANGSTA I II III IV
CONFESSIONS OF A JACKBOY I II
By Nicholas Lock
I'M NOTHING WITHOUT HIS LOVE
SINS OF A THUG
TO THE THUG I LOVED BEFORE
A GANGSTA SAVED XMAS
IN A HUSTLER I TRUST
By Monet Dragun
CAUGHT UP IN THE LIFE I II III
THE STREETS NEVER LET GO I II
By Robert Baptiste
NEW TO THE GAME I II III
MONEY, MURDER & MEMORIES I II III

Gorillaz in the Trenches

By **Malik D. Rice**

LIFE OF A SAVAGE I II III

A GANGSTA'S QUR'AN I II III IV

MURDA SEASON I II III

GANGLAND CARTEL I II III

CHI'RAQ GANGSTAS I II III

KILLERS ON ELM STREET I II III

JACK BOYZ N DA BRONX I II III

A DOPEBOY'S DREAM I II III

JACK BOYS VS DOPE BOYS

COKE GIRLZ

COKE BOYS

By **Romell Tukes**

LOYALTY AIN'T PROMISED I II

By **Keith Williams**

QUIET MONEY I II III

THUG LIFE I II III

EXTENDED CLIP I II

A GANGSTA'S PARADISE

By **Trai'Quan**

THE STREETS MADE ME I II III

By **Larry D. Wright**

THE ULTIMATE SACRIFICE I, II, III, IV, V, VI

KHADIFI

IF YOU CROSS ME ONCE

ANGEL I II III

IN THE BLINK OF AN EYE

By **Anthony Fields**

THE LIFE OF A HOOD STAR

By **Ca$h & Rashia Wilson**

SAYNOMORE

THE STREETS WILL NEVER CLOSE I II III

By K'ajji

CREAM I II III

THE STREETS WILL TALK

By Yolanda Moore

NIGHTMARES OF A HUSTLA I II III

By King Dream

CONCRETE KILLA I II III

VICIOUS LOYALTY I II

By Kingpen

HARD AND RUTHLESS I II

MOB TOWN 251

THE BILLIONAIRE BENTLEYS I II III

By Von Diesel

GHOST MOB

Stilloan Robinson

MOB TIES I II III IV V VI

SOUL OF A HUSTLER, HEART OF A KILLER

GORILLAZ IN THE TRENCHES

By SayNoMore

BODYMORE MURDERLAND I II III

THE BIRTH OF A GANGSTER I II

By Delmont Player

FOR THE LOVE OF A BOSS

By C. D. Blue

MOBBED UP I II III IV

THE BRICK MAN I II III IV

THE COCAINE PRINCESS I II III IV V

By King Rio

Gorillaz in the Trenches

KILLA KOUNTY I II III

By Khufu

MONEY GAME I II

By Smoove Dolla

A GANGSTA'S KARMA I II

By FLAME

KING OF THE TRENCHES I II

by **GHOST & TRANAY ADAMS**

QUEEN OF THE ZOO I II

By **Black Migo**

GRIMEY WAYS I II

By Ray Vinci

XMAS WITH AN ATL SHOOTER

By Ca$h & Destiny Skai

KING KILLA

By Vincent "Vitto" Holloway

BETRAYAL OF A THUG

By Fre$h

THE MURDER QUEENS I II

By Michael Gallon

TREAL LOVE

By Le'Monica Jackson

FOR THE LOVE OF BLOOD

By Jamel Mitchell

HOOD CONSIGLIERE

By Keese

PROTÉGÉ OF A LEGEND

By Corey Robinson

BORN IN THE GRAVE

By Self Made Tay

SAYNOMORE

MOAN IN MY MOUTH
By XTASY

BOOKS BY LDP'S CEO, CA$H

TRUST IN NO MAN

TRUST IN NO MAN 2

TRUST IN NO MAN 3

BONDED BY BLOOD

SHORTY GOT A THUG

THUGS CRY

THUGS CRY 2

THUGS CRY 3

TRUST NO BITCH

TRUST NO BITCH 2

TRUST NO BITCH 3

TIL MY CASKET DROPS

RESTRAINING ORDER

RESTRAINING ORDER 2

IN LOVE WITH A CONVICT

LIFE OF A HOOD STAR

XMAS WITH AN ATL SHOOTER

SAYNOMORE